THE WHITE WITCH

"What can I do? What the Devil can I do?"

The Marquis spoke the words aloud.

As he said them, he knew that Locadi was thinking of him and willing him towards her. It was then that he was struck with a sudden idea.

If Locadi was using black magic which was evil, the only antidote would be something good.

For a moment he thought of riding over to see Flora and asking for her help, but then he told himself that was impossible.

She must certainly not become involved in anything like his present situation. She is pure, good and, he suspected, very innocent.

How could she understand women like Locadi who aroused passions in a man that were purely physical?

And yet had nothing to do with the spiritual side of love.

'*Good and bad! Bad and good*!'

The words seemed to repeat themselves in his brain.

THE BARBARA CARTLAND PINK COLLECTION

Titles in this series

THE WHITE WITCH

BARBARA CARTLAND

Barbaracartland.com Ltd

Copyright © 2006 by Cartland Promotions

First published on the internet in August 2006 by
Barbaracartland.com

ISBN 1-905155-22-0

ISBN 978-1-905155-22-4

Printed and bound in Great Britain by CLE Print Ltd. of
St Ives, Cambridgeshire.

THE BARBARA CARTLAND PINK COLLECTION

Barbara Cartland was the most prolific bestselling author in the history of the world. She was frequently in the Guinness Book of Records for writing more books in a year than any other living author. In fact her most amazing literary feat was when her publishers asked for more Barbara Cartland romances, she doubled her output from 10 books a year to over 20 books a year, when she was 77.

She went on writing continuously at this rate for 20 years and wrote her last book at the age of 97, thus completing 400 books between the ages of 77 and 97.

Her publishers finally could not keep up with this phenomenal output, so at her death she left 160 unpublished manuscripts, something again that no other author has ever achieved.

Now the exciting news is that these 160 original unpublished Barbara Cartland books are ready for publication and they will be published by Barbaracartland.com exclusively on the internet, as the web is the best possible way to reach so many Barbara Cartland readers around the world.

The 160 books will be published monthly and will be numbered in sequence.

The series is called the Pink Collection as a tribute to Barbara Cartland whose favourite colour was pink and it became very much her trademark over the years.

The Barbara Cartland Pink Collection is published only on the internet. Log on to www.barbaracartland.com to find out how you can purchase the books monthly as they are published, and take out a subscription that will ensure that all subsequent editions are delivered to you by mail order to your home.

If you do not have access to a computer you can write for information about the Pink Collection to the following address :

Barbara Cartland.com Ltd.
Camfield Place,
Hatfield,
Hertfordshire AL9 6JE
United Kingdom.

Telephone : +44 (0)1707 642629
Fax :   +44 (0)1707 663041

THE LATE DAME BARBARA CARTLAND

Barbara Cartland who sadly died in May 2000 at the age of nearly 99 was the world's most famous romantic novelist who wrote 723 books in her lifetime with worldwide sales of over 1 billion copies and her books were translated into 36 different languages.

As well as romantic novels, she wrote historical biographies, 6 autobiographies, theatrical plays, books of advice on life, love, vitamins and cookery. She also found time to be a political speaker and television and radio personality.

She wrote her first book at the age of 21 and this was called *Jigsaw*. It became an immediate bestseller and sold 100,000 copies in hardback and was translated into 6 different languages. She wrote continuously throughout her life, writing bestsellers for an astonishing 76 years. Her books have always been immensely popular in the United States, where in 1976 her current books were at numbers 1 & 2 in the B. Dalton bestsellers list, a feat never achieved before or since by any author.

Barbara Cartland became a legend in her own lifetime and will be best remembered for her wonderful romantic novels, so loved by her millions of readers throughout the world.

Her books will always be treasured for their moral message, her pure and innocent heroines, her good looking and dashing heroes and above all her belief that the power of love is more important than anything else in everyone's life.

"Eternal love – I have always believed that real true love lasts beyond this life and into the next."

Barbara Cartland

CHAPTER ONE
1866

"Excuse me, my Lord, but I found this in your evening-coat."

The Marquis of Wynstanton looked down at the object his valet was holding in his hand. It was a strange-looking round stone with carvings on it and there were recesses cut in its surface which seemed somewhat like eyes.

For a moment the Marquis was inclined to say that it was only rubbish and should be thrown away. But he took it from his valet asking,

"You say this was in my evening-coat?"

"Yes, my Lord, in one of the tails."

The Marquis looked surprised.

He was aware, but did not say so, that it must have been pressed in through a gap in the stitching at the top or the side of a tail, as there was no obvious opening such as a pocket.

Then because his valet was looking at him expectantly he said,

"Put it down please and I will look at it later." He finished dressing, taking trouble over his tie and making certain that everything about his attire was neat and correct.

He was conscious of the fact that he was considered not only one of the most handsome men in London but one of the best dressed.

It was indeed a compliment that he appreciated. When he was finally ready, he picked up the stone his valet had found and carrying it in his hand, he walked downstairs to his study.

It was an attractively furnished room, as were all the rooms in his house in Grosvenor Square. The pictures on the walls were exceptionally fine and exquisitely painted.

The Marquis was frowning as he sat down at his Regency desk with its flat top and polished brass feet.

He placed the small stone on his blotting-pad and stared at it.

He recognized instantly exactly what it was. On one of his travels and he had travelled a great deal around the world, he had visited Haiti. He was quite certain that what his valet had found in his coat tail was a charm or talisman from that particular country.

When he thought it over he realized who had secreted it there and for what purpose.

He had been pursued by Lady Marshall for a long time before he finally succumbed to her insistent entreaties and had become her lover.

Her husband, Lord Marshall, was obsessed by the sport of fishing. He spent much of his time going from river to river in England and Scotland to catch salmon, trout or any other fish that was available.

His very beautiful wife, being left alone in London, not surprisingly granted her favours to the many men who pursued her.

She was certainly outstanding amongst the 'professional' beauties – as they were called – who were to be found at Marlborough House.

The Prince of Wales had set the current fashion for gentlemen to pursue beautiful ladies of their own class, after he had met Lily Langtry.

Until then, it was considered correct for gentlemen like the Marquis to keep a mistress, not of his own class, in a discreet little house in Regents Park or Chelsea.

There was no question of the mistresses parading such *affaires de coeur* in the social world.

Of course there were secret liaisons in Society, but they were in fact kept very secret. Even the gossips who pried into everything found it difficult to be certain of the scandals they were whispering about.

Was it not true that the lovely Duchess of Manchester was having a love affair with Lord Harrington? Were two other acclaimed beauties actually being unfaithful to their husbands?

The Marquis was certainly not the first lover Lady Marshall had taken since her marriage. As he was exceptionally fastidious, he did not wish to follow a certain Duke whom he thought had preceded him.

Lady Marshall was however used to getting her own way. She had no intention whatever of being refused by any man on whom she had turned her strange green eyes. They were combined with brilliant dark hair with touches of blue.

Her white skin was the envy of every other London beauty.

Her slender, sinuous and exquisite figure made it difficult to believe that any man could refuse her.

The Marquis however had remained aloof in his own particular way. He consistently ignored the very obvious invitations in her eyes.

She had invited him on numerous occasions to dinner, all of which he had refused. He had however spent much time in her company at other parties.

He was not absolutely sure when he found himself invariably sitting next to her at dinner, whether it was due to her contrivance or merely to chance.

Lady Marshall had been forced to wait for nearly two months. Finally the Marquis had succumbed and accepted an invitation to what he was told was a dinner party.

When he arrived he was not really surprised to be told that the other guests had either been taken ill or called to the country.

He and his hostess were alone.

The end to the evening was inevitable.

He was forced to admit to himself when he returned home as dawn was breaking that he had not in his previous affairs encountered anyone so fiery, so insatiable or so extremely alluring.

It was two days later that he learned that Lord Marshall had been smitten with a heart attack.

He had been fishing in Scotland and, owing to the length of time it took before he could be seen by a doctor, had died.

It was obvious when the funeral was over that Lady Marshall expected the Marquis to console her.

He found her looking exceedingly beautiful. Undoubtedly the conventional black she was forced to wear accentuated the fineness of her skin and the elegance of her figure.

She wept a little on the Marquis's shoulder. There was only one obvious way to console her.

However the Marquis thought it would be a great mistake for him to allow his name to be linked with anyone so beautiful the moment she had been widowed.

He therefore set off on one of his trips abroad as there were still a few parts of the world he had not yet explored.

*

The Marquis enjoyed travelling and was even amused by the difficulties and hardships it often entailed.

This time he visited Nepal.

He found it an extremely interesting country even if the journey involved him in much effort.

Some of the accommodation where he had to stay was very primitive.

Nevertheless he felt the experience had given him new ideas and the treasures he brought back with him would certainly add to his collection at Wyn Castle, his country house.

He intended to take the ancient manuscripts, the carvings and the pictures he had collected to the country as soon as he returned to England.

But he found Lady Marshall was waiting for him in London.

Locadi, which was her unusual Christian name, made certain that having returned the Marquis could not escape her again. He was not entirely reluctant to comply, having spent so many months abroad without any female company.

There was no doubt that Locadi made their love affair exciting. She was different in so many ways from anyone the Marquis had encountered before.

Because he found anything new and unusual so attractive, he had stayed in London instead of going to Wyn Castle as he should have done.

London at that moment was particularly alluring. The golden daffodils and crimson tulips make huge patches of colour in Hyde Park. Rotten Row was filled every morning with the smartest horses that money could buy and the prettiest women to admire him whenever he appeared.

As the Season had begun there were luncheons, receptions and balls every day.

The Prince of Wales had made it quite clear, now that the Marquis had returned, that he required him as a frequent guest at Marlborough House.

Apart from the residents at the British Embassies where he stayed because they were more comfortable than hotels, the Marquis had talked only with the inhabitants of Nepal.

He had, it was true, spent a night or two with Maharajahs, as he had passed through India.

Otherwise he had been alone on his travels. He had stayed with the Viceroy in Calcutta for his last night before returning home.

His Excellency had said to him,

"I cannot imagine, Wynstanton, why you need to punish yourself by undertaking such a hazardous and uncomfortable journey."

"I have enjoyed it enormously," the Marquis replied and the Viceroy had laughed.

"One man's pleasure is another man's pain," he declared. "All I can say is I am thankful I was not travelling with you!"

The Marquis had to admit, now he was home, that he had almost forgotten how comfortable his bed was at Grosvenor Square or how delicious were the meals his French chef served him.

It was also a joy to ride one of his spirited and well-bred horses every morning. As a means of transport they were very different from the reluctant mules which so often in Nepal had been the only animals available, or the uncomfortably lumpy trains which had carried him across India.

It was therefore not surprising that he enjoyed the softness of Locadi's body, the exotic fragrance of the scent she always used, and the words of love she murmured against his lips.

It was an enchantment he had forgone for too long.

*

Yet now the Marquis was decidedly frowning at the object his valet had found.

Being extremely astute he had learned in his travels a great deal about witchcraft.

He therefore realised that what the valet had found in his coat was indeed a magic talisman. It was used in Haiti to evoke love in those who carried it.

It only confirmed his suspicions that Locadi Marshall wanted to marry him.

Now he thought about it, he had noticed that when he dined with her since his return from Nepal, she had always placed an orchid in his buttonhole.

He had thought it rather touching that she should take so much trouble.

When he left her presence however he always removed the orchid. He did not really care to appear with a buttonhole, whatever flower it might be.

He remembered that because of the formation of the tubers and flowers of the orchid it was frequently used in aphrodisiac love potions. The flower was regarded as a symbol of sex in many works of art.

Quite simply Locadi was using magic to attract him. He had no idea how much she might know about the subject nor had it ever occurred to him in his wildest dreams that anyone would try to arouse his love by witchcraft.

Thinking it over he became even more suspicious.

It was not only the way that Locadi behaved when they were making love. It was not just the talisman he held in his hand.

7

It was, he realised, as if she was attempting to intrude into his mind.

When he was with her he had found himself occasionally, when he least expected it, thinking of marriage.

He had however, some time before he had met Locadi, when his family had begged and pleaded with him, made up his mind.

He would not marry for a long time.

Firstly because it would inevitably curtail his travelling, which he enjoyed above all else and secondly because he had no wish to be faithful to one woman when he could choose from so many.

He would have been stupid, which he was not, if he had not been aware of his value. With his social position, his wealth and his good looks, he was an extremely desirable partner for any woman.

He fully appreciated that it was his duty eventually to produce a son and heir and he was quite prepared to do so – but later in life.

What he desired most at the moment was to be free to go to Nepal or any other part of the world which attracted him without the need to worry that he was neglecting a wife.

Worse still if he might even have to take her with him!

He had often thought and even said jokingly that in his last incarnation he had been an explorer.

"It must have been in the days," he said, "when there was a great deal more of the world to discover than there is now. I am quite certain I would have travelled to strange places like Tibet, darkest Africa, and undoubtedly made an attempt on the North Pole."

Those who heard him say this laughed and considered it a great joke.

But to the Marquis there was much truth in this thought.

He wanted to remain a bachelor and he did not wish to be shackled in any way.

The very idea of marriage made him remove himself quickly and definitely from any female who might have been suggesting it.

He thought now that he had been very stupid in not realising that Locadi had never been satisfied with being married to an unimportant Peer who had very little money.

The Marquis was not quite certain what her standing had been before she married. He imagined that Lord Marshall was the best amongst her suitors and so she had accepted him.

But he had been a great deal older than her, although at least as his wife she was able to appear at the Opening of Parliament and to be accepted by the social world.

Marriage!

The Marquis found himself almost shivering at the idea.

If he must marry, as he would eventually have to, it was certainly not going to be to someone like Locadi.

A woman whom he could not trust if she was out of his sight. Now as he thought it over, he was more convinced that ever that she was determined to capture him.

It was not only the charm from Haiti that worried him or the orchids.

He thought that some of the food he had eaten in Locadi's house might have contained an aphrodisiac, which had made their lovemaking even more passionate.

At the time he had just attributed it to the fact that he had been abroad and celibate for so long. Or perhaps the wine he had drunk at dinner had been particularly stimulating.

Now he was dubious.

He gazed at the small object lying on his blotter.

He recognised that any Priest of the voodoo in Haiti could supply this type of magic. There were many substances which their charms might contain or be treated with.

The most alarming being the blood of a newly born child.

There was no fire in the Marquis's study as the weather was warm, so he lit the small candle on his desk which he used for sealing his letters.

Then he had a better idea.

He remembered someone telling him that if you accidentally broke a mirror you should throw the broken pieces into deep water. This ensured that you would not suffer the bad luck that would be expected otherwise.

The Marquis had laughed at such superstition. But he had been assured that it was definitely true and neither good luck nor bad would ensue if the object was drowned.

'I will throw it into the Serpentine,' the Marquis told himself, 'and there it can do no one any harm.'

Then and there he decided he would go to the country.

He felt no desire to meet Locadi and find himself in a position where she could ask him why his affections had changed. He did not wish to touch her again nor even to see her again.

She was using black magic to attract him and the sooner he was completely rid of her the better.

He did however recognise that it was going to be extremely difficult.

Therefore his best solution to this problem was to leave London for the country. If he had not just come back from a long journey, he might have gone abroad again.

However he now wanted to stay in England and to see

his racehorses compete in some of the Classic races for which they had already been entered.

The most prestigious was the Derby, which would take place in ten days time. Later he hoped, if he was lucky, he would win the Gold Cup at Ascot.

*

As was usual, having made up his mind, the Marquis wasted no time. He rang the bell and having sent for his secretary started to issue his orders.

"You do realise, my Lord," his secretary told him, "that you have not visited the castle for over a year."

"I know that, Barratt," the Marquis replied, "but I expect to find everything in perfect order."

"I am sure Mr. Potter will have seen to that, my Lord," Mr. Barratt replied, "but at the same time he would wish to receive notice of your impending arrival."

The Marquis considered for a moment before responding,

"I think that would be a mistake. If all my instructions have been carried out as they should have been, even though I was abroad, they should be ready for me to arrive at any moment without a fanfare of trumpets to warn them."

"I hope you are right, my Lord. Actually I have not heard from Mr. Potter for some time, although he did write to me soon after you left for abroad to say that everything was in good order."

"That is all I need to know" the Marquis replied. "I will journey in my travelling-carriage drawn by the four horses I bought at Tattersall's just before I left for Nepal."

"Very good, my Lord, and will you be leaving tomorrow morning?"

"I am leaving in an hour's time," the Marquis decided, "so please instruct Wilkins to have everything packed and he of course will accompany me."

Mr. Barratt almost ran from the room.

'It is just like the Marquis' he thought, 'to make up his mind at a moment's notice and upset everyone.'

The Marquis's father had been a leisurely man, who had suffered much ill health in his old age. He had left everything he could to those he employed.

The young Marquis was very different.

It was perhaps, Mr. Barratt believed, because of an unhappy childhood.

At the same time he has been brought up to be very conscious of his own stature and importance.

'He likes to snap his fingers and expect the world to run to do his bidding,' Mr. Barratt complained to himself as he reached his office at the back of the house, where he rang bells which made the servants come hurrying in to find out what was required.

The Marquis meantime had walked to the window overlooking the garden in the centre of Grosvenor Square.

He was not seeing the statue in the garden or the daffodils making a golden circle around it.

Instead he was seeing the Priest who had taken him to a voodoo service in Haiti, where he had watched a strange dance of those who were already 'high' on a white drink they had imbibed.

The voodoo rites were all very ancient and traditional and they always ended in an orgy which the Marquis found interesting but distinctly unpleasant.

It was undoubtedly from Haiti that Locadi had obtained her love charm.

The sooner he was rid of it the better.

The one possession he had always been very careful to preserve was his brain. He had always despised people who took drugs of any sort, including painkillers and sleeping pills.

"The most valuable blessing we possess," he had said on various occasions somewhat pompously, "is our brains. The only possibility for me to talk to you and you to talk to me is by using our brains. If our brains are damaged, we are no longer ourselves."

The gentleman to whom he was speaking had not taken him seriously.

"There is nothing wrong with your brains, Ivor," he said, "and when you produce children they will doubtless be as clever as you are and of course will tell you they know better than you!"

The Marquis however had not been listening.

He was working it out for himself how many men wasted their brains and how many were unappreciated by those around them.

He almost placed himself in the latter category, although he was well aware that everyone respected him.

Then the thought occurred to him somewhat bitterly that it was his money and his title that they respected. Not the fact he could be very much more intelligent than they were.

Now he was running away but at the same time it was the most sensible course of action.

As he thought his situation over, he remembered dreaming several nights ago of Locadi. He had seen her looking at him as if out of the frame of a picture.

If she was using magic, she was sending her thoughts to him while he was asleep.

She was willing him see her as one of the Marchionesses of Wynstanton whose portraits hung on the walls in Grosvenor Square and his other houses.

She wanted to marry him and was therefore using

every ploy to make him see her as his wife.

'I must escape,' the Marquis told himself, but he did not feel that he was being a coward.

He had seen too much of magic as he had travelled around the world not to appreciate that in the wrong hands it could be very dangerous.

It was not just the voodoo in Haiti which frightened him, there was also the same magic to be found in every country in the East.

Sometimes in India it had seemed quite harmless. One of his servants there had told him that he wished to leave immediately as his father had died.

"How do you know?" the Marquis asked.

He knew the man's father lived in Calcutta, and they were at that moment five hundred miles away.

"My father dead, Lord say it," the Indian had replied. "Family call for me. I go to them."

Because he was a good servant, the Marquis had been extremely annoyed at losing his services.

However because he was so obviously upset by his father's supposed death and determined that he must support his family, the Marquis had permitted him to leave.

It was several months later when he had returned to Calcutta and saw the man again.

He learned that his father had indeed died on exactly the night he had known about it. He was very grateful to the Marquis for allowing him return to his family.

There was no possible way he could have been informed of his father's death except through his mind and intuition.

The Marquis had puzzled over this phenomenon and found the whole subject most interesting. It was something he would like to experiment with himself one day.

It never occurred to him that a woman might use such thought transference on him or that she could make him think of her as his wife.

He could perhaps be mesmerised, if that was the right word, into doing what she wanted.

'I must retreat and think this situation through clearly, the Marquis told himself.

He was waiting impatiently in the hall while his travelling-carriage was being brought to the door.

His valet, Wilkins, and the luggage were travelling in another carriage and would therefore arrive later at the castle.

It was more usual, as Mr. Barratt had pointed out, for the servants to go ahead and prepare for the Marquis's arrival.   He only hoped that his Lordship would not in consequence be too uncomfortable.

"I daresay I shall manage," the Marquis said with a smile.

"I should have brought it to your Lordship's notice earlier," Mr. Barratt continued, "that you permitted your grandmother, the Dowager Marchioness, to stay at the castle, as she wished to do, a week ago."

The Marquis stared at him.

"I had indeed forgotten, Barratt. Do you mean to say that her Ladyship is there now?"

"I am not quite sure, my Lord. If you remember her Ladyship wrote to you saying that she was suffering from various ailments, which her doctors thought might be alleviated if she stayed in the country now that the weather has improved."

"Yes, yes of course, now I remember." The Marquis did recall as he spoke that the letter had arrived at the moment when he was hurrying to be with Locadi. She had sent a message to welcome him home and to say that she was counting the minutes until she would see him again.

It had been a beguiling message. A mixture of pleading and passion that the Marquis had found difficult to ignore.

He had not forgotten her stunning beauty on his travels, nor her passionate kisses.

He had taken a carriage to her house in Lowndes Square. When he walked into her drawing room, he believed that she was undoubtedly the most glorious woman he had ever seen.

As the butler closed the door behind him he had just stood gazing at her. With the swiftness of a serpent she had glided towards him and into his arms. She raised both hands and pulled his head down to hers. Her kiss had sent the blood throbbing in the Marquis's temples.

"I have missed you, oh, darling Ivor, how much I have missed you," Locadi murmured.

After that introduction he had forgotten everything except her and her sinuous body.

Looking back, it was from that moment he thought that he had seemed to see her face wherever he went and she haunted his dreams.

It was not that she ever mentioned anything about marriage, she was too clever for that. But it became increasingly apparent that she was exercising a subtle influence over him that made it impossible for him to think of anything but her.

'I was a fool not to realise it was abnormal,' the Marquis chastised himself.

*

The Marquis was driving with an expertise which made his groom look at him admiringly. He was

16

concentrating on the road and driving his horses faster and faster.

Yet he was still acutely conscious that Locadi was thinking of him and he could almost see her green eyes looking at him through the hedges on either side of the road. He could hear her voice in the rumble of the wheels.

He was driving so fast that his groom began to regard him nervously.

'I shall not be able to fight this problem with fear,' he thought.

He found himself wondering what was the antidote to black magic. Even if he knew what it was, where could he find it?

Wyn Castle was fortunately not very far from London.

Knowing that it would only take him under three hours to reach it, the Marquis was ashamed that he had not been there for so long.

The castle had been in the family for several centuries. It had been refaced and enlarged during the reign of George IV. It was not therefore the perfect Palladian mansion which the Marquis would have preferred.

Nevertheless the castle was an extremely impressive building. The tower had been built in Norman times and was listed in every guide book of Britain.

As it was spring the gardens should now be particularly spectacular.

Although he employed a good number of gardeners it had been worth every penny, the Marquis thought.

Fountains had been added, a bowling green and a shrubbery which was a joy to wander in.

The castle itself was a treasure house which he valued above all.

The pictures which had been collected by his ancestors

down the centuries were magnificent and rivalled those in the National Gallery.

The French furniture in two of the rooms had been bought at the time of the French Revolution. They had been brought to England at the same time that the Prince Regent had sent his chef to the sales at Versailles, because he was his only servant who could speak French.

There was also magnificent gold-framed furniture designed by Adam himself in 1750. In the study there were Regency pieces which the Prince of Wales, when he last stayed at Wyn Castle, had tried to persuade the Marquis to give to him.

He had managed to avoid doing so by telling the Prince that they were entailed.

"Of course," the Prince had conceded, "and I suppose everything else in this beautiful castle falls into the same category."

"If I was threatened with bankruptcy I would have to go through it all with a fine toothcomb to see what I could sell," the Marquis had replied. "But for the moment that uncomfortable situation has not arisen."

The Prince had laughed.

"I am sure you are quite safe," he said, "and the next generation will envy your sons in the same way that I am envying you."

The Marquis had been pleased with the compliment.

He had arranged an excellent party for the Prince with a number of very ravishing women. Everyone who played host to the Heir to the Throne understood that the Prince was quickly bored.

When this happened, he tapped his fingers on the table and looked round impatiently. It was as if he expected a new amusement to spring up from the floor or drop down from the ceiling.

To the Marquis's satisfaction the Prince did not give any sign of being bored while he had been staying at the castle. Instead he enjoyed the meals and admired the pictures and furniture.

'I suppose,' the Marquis thought, 'that now I shall have to invite His Royal Highness again, but for the moment I just want to think and wonder what I can do about Locadi.'

He was well aware she would fight desperately to hold him and would undoubtedly continue to use black magic in the attempt to capture him completely.

'I would not marry her if she was the only woman in the world,' the Marquis told himself positively.

At the same time he was alarmed. He had seen black magic at work and it was not to be taken lightly.

But genuine black magic was something very different from the activities of the poor old women who had been hanged as witches. They had invariably been tortured into making a confession.

Every European country had been abominably cruel to old women who were thought to be witches. It was a disgraceful attitude of which no one, including the Church, could be proud. That superstition, as the Marquis believed, was very different from the threat he was now encountering.

He was almost convinced that Locadi was using the black magic of Haiti on him and he had been foolish enough not to realise that her name was a very common one in that country.

She had used it because people had found it attractive and unusual in England.

If he had been more alert, he should have seen the red light warning him of danger when they had first met.

'I have to break and resist the spell she is casting over me,' the Marquis mused as he drew near to the castle.

At the same time he had no idea of how he could do so. If he had been in Haiti, in India or Nepal, he could have turned to someone wise in the knowledge of magic to help him. But where were such experts likely to be found in England?

He could imagine, if he sought advice in White's Club, how he would arouse the laughter of his friends and they would tease him unmercifully.

'No one in this country,' he thought, 'would take me seriously. They would never consider it possible that black magic could be a menace to me or anyone else.'

Amongst the country folk there would certainly be an acknowledged witch, who could have cursed the farmer if a calf was born dead. She would be consulted by the village girls when they wanted to be married.

The gypsies, he remembered, offered special cherry stones. If a girl wore them round her neck the man she had chosen would ask her to be his wife.

But Locadi was using something much more deadly than cherry stones.

The Marquis suddenly thought he had no wish to leave the sinister stone anywhere on his estate, even under water.

He remembered they would be crossing a river very shortly. To his groom's surprise he drew his team to a standstill just before they crossed the bridge.

He handed the man the reins.

"I want to go and take a look at the river," he informed him briefly.

He walked ahead onto the narrow red brick bridge which had spanned that particular river for at least a hundred years.

There had been a certain amount of rain the previous month and the water was fairly high. The Marquis leaned over the bridge and looked down into the water.

He drew Locadi's magic stone from his pocket. He took another look at it and was quite certain that it came from Haiti.

The eyes which seemed to stare at him had been packed with a powder which he was sure contained special ingredients for making a man who carried the stone fall deeply in love.

He surmised, although he was not sure, that the plants from which the powder came were somehow connected with Venus, who was invariably used when it was a question of unrequited love.

The Marquis also mused that the mandrake plant had always been believed to be endowed with mysterious powers for good and evil.

Perhaps there was something else that was hidden behind the eyes, which still seemed to stare at him.

Whatever the object was, whatever it contained, he only knew that he must be rid of it. Raising his arm he threw the stone into the very middle of the river.

It sank with hardly a splash as it was so small.

He felt as if he had cleansed himself of a heavy burden and was for the moment free.

'If I go on thinking like this,' he told himself angrily, 'I shall soon become as mad as Locadi who believes that this stone would achieve her nefarious ends.'

He turned away from the river and walked back to his carriage, and without saying a word he climbed back into the driving-seat and took the reins from the groom.

Then as the horses started off he said to himself,

'Now I am going home to my castle to everything that is familiar and sane.'

CHAPTER TWO

The Marquis pulled his horses to a standstill with a flourish and handed the reins to the groom. He stepped out and walked slowly up the steps to the front door of the castle.

It was a most impressive entrance with the steps ending at the Wynstanton crest carved in marble. The house itself was enormous and magnificent. The original castle with its tower, which was built in Norman times, formed one wing of the centre block.

The other wing had been added in the reign of George I and balanced the whole structure. The castle had been in the family for many generations.

The Marquis had spent his childhood here, but when he grew up he had preferred his other houses.

He was far happier in the house he owned in Leicestershire where he hunted with the very best packs in the County.

He also enjoyed staying at Newmarket where his racehorses were trained on his own estate which was in sight of the Racecourse.

He pulled at the bell and it seemed to him there was a long delay before the doors opened. He appreciated that this was because he was not expected. At the same time it irritated him that any caller should be kept waiting.

When the door finally opened he saw the old butler,

Bowles, who had been at the castle ever since he could remember.

"Good afternoon, Bowles," the Marquis said, "I know you are not expecting me, but I have come to see how you all are, and Wilkins is just behind me with the luggage."

Bowles gasped with astonishment before he said,

"It's very nice to see you back, Master Ivor – I means my Lord – but us weren't told you was coming."

"I am fully aware of that," the Marquis replied, "but I understand my grandmother is here?"

"Yes indeed, my Lord. Her Ladyship is upstairs and Miss Flora be with her."

"I will tell her myself about my arrival," the Marquis said. "I suppose she is in one of the State bedrooms?"

"Queen Anne's, my Lord. We thinks her Ladyship be more comfortable there and the room has the morning sun."

"That was very sensible of you, Bowles," the Marquis said as he started up the stairs.

The staircase was magnificent and the pictures which hung on either side were all of the Marquis's family. Every Earl and later every Marquis, who inherited the title had been painted by the most famous artist of his day, starting with Holbein, followed by Van Dyck, Sir Joshua Reynolds and a series of other Masters up to the present day.

The Marquis was thinking as he reached the top of the stairs that he would be wise to be painted himself while he was still young.

Some of his ancestors had waited until they were almost in their dotage, but the ladies had been far wiser. They had been painted at the height of their beauty.

He appreciated one especially beautiful Countess as he walked along the corridor.

He then remembered that Locadi was determined to join them.

With a shudder he hurried on to the State room where his grandmother was to be found.

She had been acknowledged a great beauty in her youth. She was still, the Marquis remembered when he had last seen her, very beautiful.

He knocked on the door.

It was opened by an elderly lady's maid and the Marquis asked,

"Is her Ladyship prepared to see me?"

Before he had finished speaking, there was a cry of "Ivor!" from the bed.

He walked forward to see his grandmother looking very regal against a pile of lace-trimmed pillows.

"My dear boy!" she exclaimed, "how delightful to see you! I had no idea you were coming home."

"I had no idea myself until a few hours ago," the Marquis replied. He reached the bed and bent to kiss his grandmother before he added,

"I only found out as I was leaving that you were staying here."

"I came because I was suffering so desperately with rheumatism," the Dowager Marchioness explained.

"Although I have been here only a short time, Flora has done wonders for me and I feel so much better than I have for a long time."

As she spoke the Marquis glanced at a young woman who had moved to one side as he approached the bed.

He saw that she was young and was wearing a white apron. It made him think she was one of the servants.

"I am so glad you are feeling better, Grandmama," he said. "It is delightful to find you here when I expected I would be alone."

"I am waiting to hear all about your travels," the

Dowager answered. "They tell me that you have not been here for a very long time."

"I am sure that will be said to me over and over again," the Marquis replied with a twinkle. "So please, Grandmama, do not reproach me and let us enjoy ourselves now that I am definitely back in residence."

The Dowager gave a laugh.

"I am feeling so much better thanks to Flora," she said, "so I may even be able to join you at dinner."

"I should give it another day or two," the girl called Flora counselled quietly.

The Marquis thought that this was the sort of interference that annoyed him.

If his grandmother felt well enough to come down to dinner, then that was what she should do. It would be a great mistake to listen to gloomy servants who always made out someone who was ill to be worse than they actually were.

To his grandmother he said, "we will talk about it later when we are alone."

"I am leaving now," Flora remarked before the Dowager could speak. "And of course I will return this evening to make you comfortable for the night."

"Thank you, dear child," the Dowager responded. "You know how grateful I am."

Flora smiled at her and taking off her apron moved across the room towards the door. She opened it and was in the passage before on an impulse the Marquis followed her.

When they were both outside he said,

"I wanted to ask you if my grandmother is really ill and, if so, why you are treating her rather than the doctor."

Flora, who now held her white apron over her arm, answered quietly,

"My treatment is rather different, my Lord, from

anything that a doctor would give her Ladyship."

"Different?" the Marquis queried. "In what way?"

"I tend a herb garden, my Lord, and it is with the right herbs for the rheumatism that your grandmother is suffering from, that I have been treating her."

"Herbs!" the Marquis exclaimed. "Do you really believe they are effective?"

"Very effective indeed, my Lord, as anyone who lives locally will tell you."

The Marquis thought of the orchids that Locadi had fastened in his buttonhole and of the herbs which were used by the Priests in Haiti.

For a moment he considered accusing this young woman of deceiving the people she treated.

It was obviously a load of skullduggery as herbs contained no real healing powers such as the pills and potions provided by the medical profession.

Instead he asked her a question,

"I suppose you are paid for what you are doing?" He thought as he spoke that the whole idea was just another way of extracting money from the rich who could afford to pay.

"Of course," Flora said, in the same quiet voice she had used before. "I ask people to contribute as much as they can afford."

The Marquis looked at her in amazement. She was at least frankly admitting that what she was doing was crooked.

"The money I obtain," Flora continued, "goes, my Lord, for pay for a teacher to come to the village three times a week now that the school has been closed."

The Marquis gazed at her.

"The school is closed?" he repeated, "Why?"

"We were told it was on your Lordship's instructions. You said it was a waste of money."

There was no doubt now of the hostility in Flora's voice.

The Marquis was staring at her in sheer astonishment.

"That is untrue," he retorted.

"You can hardly expect me to believe *that*," Flora replied, "when you also dismissed the Vicar and he left in tears. I felt that no one could be so cruel."

The Marquis was for the moment speechless.

She added as if the words burst from her lips,

"I think you are a – disgrace to – your family."

She turned round as she spoke and ran down the stairs.

Before the Marquis could stop her, she had slipped out through the front door and disappeared.

He thought he must be dreaming.

Never in his life had any woman spoken to him in such a manner and he could only imagine that she must be deranged to attribute such actions to himself.

He considered returning to his grandmother to discuss this outburst with her, before deciding that as she was old and obviously pleased with the treatment she was receiving, whatever it was, he therefore could hardly say that he thought the girl was a lunatic.

*

Instead he walked slowly downstairs and when he reached the hall the old butler came towards him.

"I was wondering, my Lord," he asked, "if you'll be requiring luncheon?"

"Yes of course I shall, Bowles," the Marquis replied.

"It'll be difficult, as the Missus has just pointed out to me, my Lord, but we'll do our best to provide you with something."

He spoke in such a worried tone that the Marquis

looked at him.

"What is worrying you, Bowles?" he enquired. "I have never known the castle lacking food and sustenance. There should be baby lamb at this time of the year and some of those delicious hams that I remember Mrs. Bowles used to cure so tastily."

"Yes, my Lord, I remembers them too," Bowles said shaking his head. "But things be very different now, very different indeed."

"In what way?" the Marquis queried.

There was a pause before Bowles replied.

"Mr. Potter allows us very little money with which to feed ourselves, and when her Ladyship arrived I had to beg the butcher and the grocer for food and the bills all need to be paid at the end of the week."

"I do not understand what you are talking about, Bowles. I recall that our provisions always came from the Home Farm and they provided us with chickens, eggs, milk, cream and anything else we required."

"Mr. Potter stopped all that, my Lord."

"Stopped it!" the Marquis exclaimed, "but why?"

There was a silence until Bowles said,

"I thinks Mr. Potter thought it were too expensive like."

"I do not know what is going on," the Marquis said sharply. "Where is Potter?"

"He is ill, my Lord, and we've not seen him for some time."

"Ill? Is he in his house?"

"Yes, my Lord."

"And you are saying that it has been difficult to buy food because Mr. Potter refuses to pay for it?"

"Yes, my Lord."

The way Bowles spoke told the Marquis that there was more to this problem than met the eye. Without saying any more he walked out through the front door and down the steps.

Potter's house where he lived as manager of the castle and estate was only a short distance from the East side of the main building, whereas his office was in the castle itself.

The Marquis wanted to find out for himself what was going on, as he still could not believe what the girl Flora and Bowles had told him.

He thought that she must have some particular grudge against Potter.

'I expect Potter will give me some reasonable explanation,' he thought to himself.

It took him only five minutes to reach the small but pretty house which was only a little larger than a cottage, and Potter had been there in his father's time and the Marquis remembered him as a rather pompous little man.

The Marquis thought he rather enjoyed ordering about the servants who were under his control.

When the Marquis reached the house he saw that the door was open.

He knocked but there was no reply.

He tried to remember whether Potter was a married man or not. If he was, there was no sign of his wife nor of anyone else.

After waiting a short while, the Marquis walked in.

The cottage which had been built about thirty years ago was identical to others his father had constructed in the village.

The staircase ended in what was a minute hall and there was a small room on either side of it and a kitchen at the far end.

The Marquis opened the door on the right into a room which was fitted up more or less as an office. There were a number of books, papers and tin boxes marked with the names of farms or other parts of the estate.

He thought that all these should have been in the estate office in the castle and he wondered why Potter had removed them to his own house.

He then opened the other door and found what he was seeking.

Seated in an armchair in front of the fireplace, although there was no fire, was Potter.

The Marquis supposed that he was asleep, but as he entered the room and drew nearer, he became aware of a very strong smell of whisky. There was a half empty bottle on the table beside Potter's chair.

The Marquis looked down at him and noted that he was indeed asleep, but it was a sleep of drunkenness. There was no doubt about it that Potter was extremely drunk.

He had raised one leg up onto a stool and from its appearance the Marquis was sure he was suffering from gout.

He looked round the room. There were two empty bottles of whisky on the table within reach of his chair and there was a case of full bottles by the window at the far end of the room.

The Marquis stood looking at Potter for a few moments and realised that it would be impossible to shake him into wakefulness.

He therefore walked towards the door, but instead of leaving the cottage he turned into the room he had visited first.

There was a large ledger on the writing-desk which stood by the window. The Marquis opened it and recognised that it was an account of the rents which had been paid on the estate.

He checked all the rents and soon noticed that they had all been increased during the last year while he had been away from the castle.

A little lower down there was a note of the amount of money that had been paid to his solicitor at the end of the month.

It only took the Marquis a brief glance to appreciate that it was very much less than that which had been collected in rents.

There was no necessity for him to read any more. Now he knew he needed to find someone who could tell him the truth about what had been happening on his estate.

Instinctively, until he was quite certain of the facts, the Marquis did not wish to discuss the matter with his servants.

He had left Potter in charge.

The man had the right to justify his actions before being accused of embezzlement.

He walked back to the castle and when he reached the hall it was to find Bowles waiting for him.

"Luncheon is served, my Lord," he announced, "I'm afraid you'll find it somewhat scrappy as the Missus says she cannot make bricks without straw."

"What you are saying, Bowles, is that as Mr. Potter is ill you are short of money?"

"Very short indeed, my Lord," Bowles answered.

The Marquis took a ten pound note out of his notecase.

"Buy what you require for dinner," he ordered, "and tomorrow I will see to it that my affairs are better organised."

"Thank you, my Lord, thank you very much," Bowles said. "It's been hard, awful hard during the time your Lordship's been away."

It struck the Marquis that Bowles was looking not only

older since he had last seen him, but also extremely thin.

"Are you telling me that you and Mrs. Bowles have not had enough to eat?" he asked sharply.

"Mr. Potter has on your instructions, my Lord, reduced the wages of everyone who works on the estate and ours were halved."

The Marquis drew in his breath.

It suddenly struck him that since he had come home he had not seen any servants except Bowles.

"What has happened to the footmen?" he asked.

"Mr. Potter dismissed them, my Lord, saying they were not wanted while you were abroad. And I do not wish to worry your Lordship as you've only just arrived, but it's very difficult for me to manage without any help."

"Has Mrs. Bowles any help in the kitchen?" the Marquis enquired.

"No, my Lord."

"Then as soon as you have served me my luncheon," the Marquis replied, walking towards the dining room, "I want you to go down into the village and bring back everyone you can who was here before I left, or fill their places as best as you can."

He noticed the old man's eyes light up and then the Marquis took several notes out of his case.

"Pay all the outstanding bills, Bowles," he said, "and tell the butcher and whoever is now running the other shops that I want everything to return to exactly as it was in my father's time."

"That's good news, very good news indeed, my Lord," Bowles muttered in a shaky voice.

The Marquis was half afraid that he would burst into tears as he sat down at the table.

"Now quickly serve me what your wife has cooked,"

he said in a different tone of voice, "and I do hope that her Ladyship is enjoying your wife's excellent cooking."

What was produced for luncheon was definitely edible but there was very little of it.

The Marquis had the uncomfortable feeling that the Bowles family would go hungry if he consumed everything that was put in front of him.

He had nearly finished what was provided when he asked,

"Who is the young woman I found in her Ladyship's room when I went upstairs? She is called Flora."

"Oh, that be Miss Romilly," Bowles replied, "Your Lordship must remember Mr. Fredrick Romilly who writes books and lives at the *Four Gables*."

"Yes of course I remember him," the Marquis said in surprise. "Are you telling me that Miss Flora is Mr. Romilly's daughter?"

"Yes, my Lord. Her were just a child before you spent so much time in London. When her mother died, she looked after the herb garden and people comes from all over the County for her to cure their ailments."

"You believe that is possible?" the Marquis asked.

"Indeed it is, my Lord," Bowles replied. "Miss Flora be wonderful in what she does for them that's old and the children what hurts themselves."

The Marquis mentally questioned this assertion.

At the same time he recalled that Fredrick Romilly had written several books which had been acclaimed in the newspapers and he would be able to tell him the truth about what was happening.

The Marquis did not believe that the school had really been closed on an order from him, as they had been told, nor that the Vicar had left because he did not receive his stipend.

That must be an absurd exaggeration on the part of the girl called Flora, but her father was a sensible and respected man.

*

The Marquis ordered a chaise to drive to the village while wondering apprehensively if his horses were still in the stables.

To his relief he learnt that Gower, the head groom, was still in charge.

The Marquis shook him by the hand before asking, "I was worried in case anything had happened to my horses whilst I was away."

"Three of them were sold, my Lord," Gower replied.

"Three?" the Marquis queried. "On whose orders?"

"Mr. Potter's, my Lord. He said he'd had your instructions as it was a mistake for us to have to feed so many."

The Marquis's lips tightened. He knew he must talk to Fredrick Romilly first before he could denounce Potter.

He took Gower with him because he did not like to ask if he still had any assistants left in the stable. They drove off down the long oak lined drive.

When they reached the lodges the Marquis enquired, "Why are they both empty?"

There was a pause before Gower answered,

"Mr. Potter refused to pay them, my Lord. He said as there'd be no one calling at the castle there was no reason for them to open the gates."

"So they went elsewhere," the Marquis said sharply.

"They couldn't stay without any wages, my Lord."

The Marquis was silent.

They drove through the iron gates which needed

repairing and their points regilding.

He noticed in the village street that the cottages were in a bad state of repair. Most of them were thatched and because the thatch had not been renewed or tended to, large parts of the roofs had been covered with pieces of tarpaulin. On some of the roofs there was old carpet or empty sacks.

He said nothing, but he missed very little as they drove down the road.

On one side there was the Park and on the other the cottages and two small shabby-looking shops. It was obvious, the Marquis thought, that no shopkeeper would stay where there was little money to be spent.

He remembered, now he thought of it, that the *Four Gables*, Fredrick Romilly's house, was at the far end of the village.

Being Elizabethan, the house was built of red brick which had mellowed over the centuries into a pink hue.

It was quite a large house with its diamond-paned windows and large gables from which it was named and so made it attractive. The strangely shaped Elizabethan chimneys enhanced its appearance.

There was a short drive and as it ended the Marquis became aware that the garden was filled with spring flowers.

The almond and cherry trees were in blossom and the whole property looked very different to everything he had just seen in the village.

Gower climbed down to knock on the front door which was opened by a neatly dressed servant. She was wearing a starched lace cap and a white apron over her dark gown which was also trimmed with lace.

The Marquis left the chaise and walked to the door.

"I wish to see Mr. Fredrick Romilly," he said, "if he is available."

"I thinks, my Lord," the maid replied dropping a little curtsy, "that the Master said he was not to be disturbed, but Miss Flora be in the drawing room."

The Marquis hesitated but then he thought it would be rude just to drive away.

He therefore followed the maid who was already leading him towards the drawing room.

When she opened the door the Marquis saw that it was a most attractive room. It was furnished with antiques in keeping with the low ceiling and the diamond-paned windows.

Sitting at the writing-table was the girl he had seen in his grandmother's bedroom.

"His Lordship be here, Miss Flora," the maid announced.

As the Marquis entered the room, he thought that Flora rose reluctantly from her desk.

Now as she waited for him to reach her, he realised that she was exceedingly pretty, perhaps lovely being the right word.

He had not noticed her looks earlier when he had believed her to be a servant.

Now he saw that her hair was the gold of the sunshine and her eyes the deep blue of cornflowers.

As he joined her, she dropped a neat curtsy saying,

"I am surprised to see your Lordship."

"I have come to see your father," the Marquis replied, "but your servant said that he was not to be disturbed. I suppose he is studying."

"Papa very much dislikes being interrupted when he is busy," Flora stated coldly. "Perhaps I can help your Lordship?"

There was no warmth in the way she spoke and the

Marquis guessed by the expression in her eyes how strongly she despised him.

It was something he could never remember happening before where a woman was concerned.

He felt annoyed that she was blaming him for sins he had not committed.

"As your father is not available, Miss Romilly," he said, "perhaps you will be kind enough to help me by answering a few questions."

This was obviously something Flora had not expected as she hesitated before responding,

"Perhaps if it is really important, I should inform Papa that you are here."

"That is not necessary," the Marquis said." I am sure, Miss Romilly, that you can assist me in his absence."

As he spoke he walked towards the fireplace. It was difficult for Flora not to follow him.

"Perhaps your Lordship would like to sit down," she offered as if she felt obliged to be polite.

"Thank you," the Marquis replied as he sat down in an armchair and after a moment's hesitation Flora sat opposite him.

There was silence until the Marquis started,

"I have just called on Mr. Potter. I suppose you and most people in the village must realise the state he is in."

"He has become gradually worse," Flora answered, "and it is not helping the people whom he has left practically starving. The cottages are falling down for want of repair and, as I have already told you, the school has been closed."

"Allow me to assure you," the Marquis asserted, "it was not on my orders. From what I have seen, Potter has been feathering his own nest at the expense of the people who were placed in his charge."

Flora looked at him.

The Marquis had a strange feeling that she was wondering if he was telling her the truth.

As if he suddenly felt he must justify himself he said,

"I assure you, Miss Romilly, that when I travelled abroad, as you may know for over a year, I expected to find everything exactly the same when I returned."

"Did you really give Mr. Potter no instructions about economy and dismissing so many men both in the house and on the estate?" Flora enquired.

"I told him to keep everything going in exactly the same way as it was when I inherited my father's title," the Marquis informed her.

Flora did not speak as he continued,

"I admit that I should have visited the castle more often before I left and on my return. But I became so involved in events that were happening in London, and it was only yesterday that I felt a sudden wish to be at Wyn."

There was a further silence before Flora said,

"I find it hard to believe that your Lordship was completely ignorant of what was happening here."

"I can only give you my word that I received no correspondence from England while I was travelling first in India and then in Nepal. When I came back to England no one told me that there had been any changes on my estate."

"How could you have been so foolish as to trust a man like Potter?" Flora asked. "Have you any idea how much he has made your people suffer? And everything that he has done to hurt or ruin them has been attributed to you."

"If that is true, I can only ask you, or rather your father, to help me put matters to right."

"I cannot allow him to be worried at this particular moment," Flora said quickly. "He is working on the most brilliant but difficult book he has ever written, and his publishers want him to finish it as quickly as possible."

She saw that the Marquis was not looking sympathetic and added pleadingly,

"Please do not disturb him. If you do so, he will believe it to be his duty to help you. Quite frankly, he has spent so much time helping the people in the village who are your responsibility, that we urgently need the money he will earn from his new book."

There was a sarcastic twist to the Marquis's lips as he replied,

"In which case, Miss Romilly, I am afraid I must ask *you* to help me."

He saw Flora stiffen and he thought for one moment that she was going to refuse him.

Then as if she realised she must not think of herself but the people who had suffered at Potter's hands, she said,

"What do you want me to do?"

"First of all I want to be put in the picture of exactly what has happened and secondly you must show me how I can make amends."

"That is a very big request, but I suppose that if your Lordship is really anxious to rectify this intolerable situation, it comes down to money and of course a little compassion on your part."

The Marquis thought as she spoke that she was sceptical as to whether he was capable of compassion.

"Thank you, Miss Romilly," he replied.

"Or shall I say Miss Flora, as that is easier? Please now tell me what I should do first."

"I should have thought that the obvious move would be to dismiss that monster, Mr. Potter, and make it quite clear to the village and everyone on your estate what you think of

39

him."

"I will certainly do just that," the Marquis said, "when he is capable of understanding me."

"Have you seen him since you arrived?"

"He was asleep or rather so drunk that he was not aware of my presence."

"He is always in that state," Flora said, "unless he is thinking out a new way of extracting money from the people ostensibly on your orders. I suspect he has put it all into his own pocket."

"From what I have seen already that would be easy to prove," the Marquis agreed. "At the same time it would cause a great scandal."

He paused before he continued, "I intend to sack Potter right away, but if I hand him over to the police it will react very unfavourably on the castle and of course on myself."

He thought as he spoke that it might also involve the gentry of the County asking awkward questions.

They could be suspicious as to why he had spent so long in London after his return from Nepal.

If he brought Locadi into the picture, she might easily twist the situation to her advantage. In fact she would say that her reputation was ruined and that she expected him to make amends by offering her marriage.

"No!" he said aloud, almost as if someone had challenged him. "Whatever happens, the least this problem is talked about the better."

"You can hardly expect people not to talk," Flora cried. "Naturally, because they have known you ever since you were born, everyone is interested in you."

She did not make her remark sound like a compliment.

"I am asking you, Miss Flora, for your help and

advice. It is too late now for recriminations."

Flora drew in her breath,

"You are making this very difficult for me. I have hated you for so long and hoped that somehow you would suffer as your people have suffered. So it is difficult to feel delighted that I can help you."

"Forget about me, and just help me to decide which people we must help first."

"Very well," Flora assented. "The pensioners have had their pension reduced by almost half. Those who were employed on the estate or in the castle were gradually sacked until there was just one left to do the work of two or three.

"As I have already told you, the school was closed on what Potter claimed were your orders, and as the Vicar received no stipend he was forced to leave."

"Will he come back?" the Marquis asked.

"As he was here for so long and knew everyone within a radius of ten miles, I think he would love to do so."

"I will double the stipend he received before," the Marquis pledged, "and also pay any expenses he incurs in moving himself and his family back into the Vicarage."

Flora clasped her hands together.

"Do you really mean that?"

"Of course I mean it," the Marquis said. "I am, as I think you know, a very rich man, and these ridiculous economies were made by Potter only because he was greedy and wished to fill his own pocket."

"I understand that now," Flora said. "But, as you know, everyone has always respected the castle, and they could not suspect that a man in such an important position could behave so dishonourably."

"I am afraid that sort of thing happens all the world over. Now what about the school?"

"It was not only closed," Flora said, "but Potter has turned it into a cottage and now charges a rent for it."

"Then we will have to build another school and quickly," the Marquis said. "In the meantime is there anywhere the children can be taught in comfort?"

Flora thought for a moment before saying,

"I have been holding a Sunday School myself in the Church, and the children have learned to sing hymns and say prayers. But that is not the same as having the Vicar amongst us."

"Of course not," the Marquis agreed, "and I think you can hardly hold school every day in the Church once the Vicar is back doing his job."

"The only place I can think of," Flora suggested tentatively, "is the castle."

The Marquis stared at her.

"Are you proposing that we should accommodate all the children in the castle?"

"There are plenty of rooms you do not use. There is the Armoury room for one, the ballroom and the music room. Perhaps there are other rooms that I have not yet seen."

"I suppose we *could* find one," the Marquis said, "and it would only be for a little while."

He felt a little reluctant to allow a large number of noisy schoolchildren into the castle.

Yet it was something that had to be done.

"If we can find the right teachers," Flora said as if she was following his thoughts, "you will experience no difficulties."

The Marquis did not argue although he wanted to do so.

"After all," Flora resumed, "some of the rooms we have just mentioned have doors opening straight into the garden. So the children would not have to come into the main house itself."

"Very well," the Marquis said. "I will leave you, Miss Flora, to choose the room you think is the most suitable. Please see to it that none of my pictures are left on the walls just in case the well-behaved children throw darts at them or think they are something to add to a bonfire!"

Flora laughed and it was a very pretty sound.

"Now your Lordship is being very imaginative. I can assure you that the idea of having lessons in the castle will leave them over-awed and talking in whispers."

"I only hope that you are right, Miss Flora." Now what else do I need to do?"

"I think, although it may sound rather presumptuous of me, that you should throw a party."

"A party!"

"To celebrate your homecoming and because you want to wipe away the hatred that is in our hearts. If you give a party like the one your father held when you were twenty-one, everyone would be thrilled and delighted."

The Marquis remembered there had been fireworks, and a huge feast had been provided in tents, where the barrels of beer and cider never ran dry. Looking back he reckoned that it was the one kindly act his father had ever done for him.

He had in fact not thrown the party to please his son, but because it would impress his neighbours, who had often thought he was very harsh with him.

The Marquis remarked that he had enjoyed the occasion to a certain extent, yet he had not been allowed to ask more than two of his friends who had studied with him at Oxford.

His father had pooh-poohed the idea of having a large

house party.

"The festivities take place outdoors and that is where they should be," his father had said. "I am not having a lot of people who bore me inside the castle."

The Marquis thought now that the village lads had enjoyed the occasion far more than he had. They had been especially thrilled by an illuminated boat, which looked like a gondola floating on the lake.

"Very well," he said aloud, "I will hold a party, but of course, Miss Flora, you must arrange it. I cannot be expected, as I am without a manager and with very few servants, to do everything myself."

Flora's eyes twinkled.

"Now I know," she said, "that you are punishing me for what I said to you. Very well, my Lord, I apologise, and I will help you make the people from the village appreciate that you are a kind, generous and friendly proprietor."

The Marquis suspected that she was laughing at him, but at the same time he understood that in the current situation he could not manage without her.

"Thank you, Miss Flora," he said, "and now just tell me how to inform everyone that their misery is over, their pensions are increased, and we need a great deal of help at the castle itself?"

"I will set the ball rolling for you," Flora replied. "You are quite certain, my Lord, that you can afford this extravagance and will not begrudge spending your money."

The Marquis looked at her sharply.

Then he realised she was being deliberately provocative.

"Of one thing I am quite certain, Miss Flora," he said as he rose to his feet, "I have engaged the right person to be in charge of all these celebrations, and that of course is – *you*."

CHAPTER THREE

The Marquis returned to the castle and was relieved to find that there were now two footmen in the hall to greet him.

He recognised both of them as having been working at the castle in the past. Their livery still fitted them and they looked very smart. He shook them both by the hand and welcomed them back.

As he walked into his study, Bowles told him there were two more men who were very willing to return, but they had however to give a week's notice to their present employer.

"I am glad they found work," the Marquis remarked.

"They were very thankful, my Lord, as their families depended on them," Bowles replied.

The Marquis climbed upstairs for a long talk with his grandmother.

She was so delighted to be feeling better and kept praising Flora for all she had done for her.

"I remember her mother possessing a gift for healing," the Dowager said, "but I believe Flora is even better. She has a magic all of her own."

The Marquis did not want to talk about magic. It was the one subject that upset him at the moment.

He was however glad to realise that despite her strong

feelings over what had been happening on the estate, Flora had not told his grandmother about the problems.

He was rather surprised because he believed that all women enjoyed chatter and gossip.

At the same time he had no wish for the Dowager to be upset as she had been suffering so much pain with her rheumatism.

Although he was alone for dinner he changed into his evening clothes.

He sat at the head of the table to be waited on by Bowles and the two footmen. The dinner was very different from his rather meagre luncheon.

He was amused to find that the main dish was a large sirloin of beef. He was quite certain that it would go, as it would have done in the old days, from the dining room to the servants hall and that night those who had been on a modest diet would be sure of a good 'tuck in'.

Because it had been along day, he was tired as he walked wearily upstairs.

However when he finally climbed into bed he found it difficult to sleep as he kept thinking of Locadi and it was almost as if she was in the room speaking to him.

'This is her magic,' he told himself as he wondered what he could do to counteract her influence.

Finally he fell asleep and he dreamed of her. When he awoke he felt again that she must by some magical power be projecting herself upon him.

He tried not to be alarmed but to think his situation out rationally, but he was forced to admit that his dilemma was becoming most unpleasant.

*

The Marquis had given orders that he would ride out before breakfast.

When he came downstairs just before seven o'clock, a horse was waiting for him in the courtyard. It was a finely built animal which was the pride of Gower's stable.

When he mounted the horse and rode off, he thought that his head groom had every reason to be pleased.

He rode for some way past fields which he thought had not been sown as they should have been by this time of the year.

In fact there were no Spring crops but only weeds on unploughed fields.

He knew that later in the day he must call on his tenant farmers. However he decided that first he would enjoy a good breakfast.

He was riding back towards the castle when he saw a horse in the distance and recognised at once that it was being ridden by a woman.

As he drew nearer he was not surprised to see it was Flora.

He felt that she was imposing on him, as she had no right to ride on his land without his permission.

As he approached her she said before he could speak,

"Good morning, my Lord. I am not trespassing as you may think but – "

"What makes you think that I may consider you a trespasser?" the Marquis interrupted.

Flora smiled.

"I am reading your thoughts and the expression in your eyes."

"If that is true," the Marquis retorted, "it is definitely something you should not be doing."

"Why?" she asked. "Are you ashamed of what you are thinking? Or have you special reasons for being secretive?"

It flashed through the Marquis's mind that he would

not like Flora to know about the trouble he was experiencing with Locadi.

Before he could answer Flora added,

"I had not finished my sentence when I said that I was not trespassing. I have been calling on Mrs. Shepherd, who if you remember was your housekeeper at the castle for many years."

"Of course I remember Mrs. Shepherd," the Marquis replied. "She was very kind to me when I was a boy. If I was sent to bed in disgrace, she always brought me up something delicious to eat."

"If you remember her that well, I am sure you will want her back now to engage housemaids and to clean the rooms on the second floor and in the wings that have not been touched for nearly a year."

"I suppose that is because Potter dismissed all the servants?"

"He sent them all away and of course Bowles and Mrs. Bowles could not do everything that was required, especially as they were kept so short of food."

"I do not want to think about it," the Marquis answered, "and of course you are quite right to ask Mrs. Shepherd to return to the castle, but will she come back?"

"She is longing to," Flora replied, "and I told her that you will send a carriage for her this afternoon as she has quite a lot of luggage and anyway she is too old to walk so far."

"Naturally I will send a carriage for her," the Marquis responded almost sharply.

He had the feeling that Flora suspected that he might be cheeseparing in some way or another.

"No I was not thinking that," she said before he could speak, "I was just afraid that you would think I was imposing on your good nature."

"Will you stop reading my thoughts!" the Marquis snapped. "They are not at all appropriate for a well brought up young woman."

Flora laughed.

"In view of all the difficulties and tragedies I have had to cope with this past year, I can assure you I am no longer a shy, ignorant *debutante*."

The Marquis laughed too because he could not help himself.

"Then what are you?" he enquired.

"The villagers call me the *White Witch*," Flora replied. "That is because I not only heal them when they are ill, but bring them luck when they are upset or in love."

"How do you do that?" the Marquis asked.

"I think a good deal of it is sheer common sense," Flora admitted frankly. "At the same time, if you believe in something strongly it makes it very much easier. And they believe in me as they believed in my mother."

She spoke quite simply and sincerely and the Marquis was impressed. It flashed through his mind that perhaps she could deal with his own particular troubles.

Then he told himself that he had no intention of becoming too familiar with any young woman.

He had always found in the past that it was the first step towards matrimony.

"I am extremely grateful, Miss Flora," he said coldly, "for all you are doing and I suggest that sometime this morning you should call at the castle to choose which room you wish to use for the schoolchildren."

"I will certainly do as you suggest, my Lord," Flora replied.

The Marquis raised his hat and rode off.

He was conscious as he did so that Flora, who had

turned in the opposite direction, looked extremely elegant on the horse she was riding.

She was moving away from him very rapidly. Compared with the London women who trit-trotted in Rotten Row just to show themselves off, she was *very* different.

When he looked back she was already almost out of sight. He wondered if he had been rude in leaving her so abruptly.

'I have to use her at the moment because there is no one else,' he mused. 'Equally I have no wish to become involved with her.'

As he ruminated, he was aware of how deeply involved he was with Locadi.

*

He enjoyed an excellent breakfast, eating all the dishes he remembered liking in the past.

When he had finished, Bowles brought in the post. There were only two letters.

One was from his secretary, Mr. Barrett.

He recognised the handwriting on the other letter all too easily.

He wondered if he should throw it away without even reading it.

Then he told himself that he was being very childish.

A letter from Locadi could not hurt him any more than he was hurt already. He could not however fail to notice, as he opened the envelope, the fragrance of the perfume she always wore.

He was not surprised to find a small orchid tucked inside with the letter, which was written in Locadi's somewhat flamboyant hand.

She wrote,

"Dearest Fascinating and Beloved Ivor, I miss you terribly. I cannot understand why you had to rush to the country without saying goodbye. Your secretary tells me that you departed on urgent business. What business could be more important than ours? Dearest Ivor, make me happy by letting me know that you will be returning very shortly. In the meantime I am thinking of you and loving you.

Locadi."

The Marquis read it again.

Going to his study he held the letter over the grate and burnt it together with the orchid into ashes.

He had an uncomfortable feeling that although he might destroy her letter, it would not stop Locadi attempting to bewitch him. She would continue to use the power of thought to make him acutely aware of her all the time.

In fact he almost felt as if she was standing beside him laughing at his endeavours to be rid of her.

Because he did not wish to think of her or what was happening to him he marched over to the stables.

He needed to inspect whichever horses remained. He also told Gower he could hire more help and that his wages were doubled.

The man was overcome.

"I don't know what to say to your Lordship," he said. "It's been real hard to carry on these past months with no help and begrudged every mouthful the horses ate."

The Marquis noticed that they were rather thin, but otherwise looked healthy. He could only thank Gower for staying and for caring for his animals as best he could.

"It were a crying shame, my Lord," he said, "that Mr. Potter sold them three. I'd been thinking that when you comes home you'd be proud to ride them."

"Then the best thing you can do," the Marquis

exclaimed, "is to buy me three more good steeds immediately and keep your eyes open for anything else that you think would be a credit to our stable."

Gower stared at him.

"Does your Lordship really mean that? I were told you intended to economise on your horses both here and at Newmarket."

The Marquis stiffened.

He had not expected that Potter would interfere with his racehorses. Was it possible that they too had been sold or deprived as his horses here at the castle had been?

"Have you any knowledge of what has been happening at Newmarket?" he asked sharply.

"I understands, my Lord," Gower replied somewhat reluctantly, "that Mr. Potter told your Lordship's manager that you were a cutting down in every direction and that he was to sell any horses that were superfluous."

"And did Saunders agree?" the Marquis enquired. He was horrified at what he had just heard and there was a harshness in his voice which Gower did not miss.

"It be all right, my Lord," he said soothingly. "Mr. Saunders I understands tells Mr. Potter he'd no instructions from your Lordship and he would not sell anything until he were told direct as it were."

"Thank God!" the Marquis cried.

He could hardly believe that Potter could have schemed so wickedly. He had devised every possible way with which to line his pockets while his Master was safely half way across the world.

When the Marquis left the stables he knew that he would have to face Potter.

He had considered sending for him, yet seeing how swollen his leg was, it was unlikely that Potter could walk so far and if he did, he might be obliged to commiserate with him.

Thinking it was an unpleasant task which could not be put off any longer, he walked again to Potter's house.

There was no sign of anyone about so he opened the door and walked in.

He half expected that having heard of his arrival, Potter would have moved into the room that he used as an office. He would be trying to hide the evidence of his crimes.

However when the Marquis opened the door, the room was exactly as it had looked yesterday. He therefore turned to the other door opposite.

Potter was still in the chair in which he had seen him with his gouty foot raised onto a footstool.

As the Marquis moved a little closer he realised with a sense of shock that the man was dead.

There was a revolver in his hand and he had shot himself through the mouth. His face was not marked and only the back of his head was shattered.

The Marquis stood looking at him. He was thinking how sad it was that any man should have to pay for his crimes in such a horrible manner.

He knew however that Potter had not thought he would return so unexpectedly. Once he had found out, there was no hiding or covering up his tracks.

In fact he had done the only possible thing he could do under the circumstances.

The Marquis left the house and returned to the stables to find Gower.

He told him what had happened and asked him to fetch the nearest doctor who lived some little distance away in another village.

Gower was shocked by the news of what had occurred but was not surprised.

"I'll be frank with your Lordship," he said, "and say that at first us believed what Mr. Potter told us."

"I can understand that," the Marquis replied.

"As things got worse," Gower continued, "us suspected that something were wrong."

Then he smiled before he said,

"I've served your Lordship and been employed at the castle for nigh on ten years. I comes here when I was a boy and I've never known your Lordship mean or stingy where an animal be concerned."

"I hope that applies to people also," the Marquis said. "I am looking to you, Gower, to try to bring the estate back to where it was before I went away."

"I'll do my best, my Lord," Gower promised.

The Marquis knew he must tell Flora what had happened before she heard the story from the village. He ordered a fresh horse to be saddled and rode off towards the *Four Gables*.

When he reached the house, a groom who had seen him riding up the drive came to hold his horse.

"If you be wanting Miss Flora, my Lord," he said, "her be in the herb garden," as he pointed the way.

The Marquis, instead of entering the house, walked across the well-kept green lawn.

He could not help thinking that Flora should be helping him rather than bothering about any herbs at this particular moment.

'They cannot be as important as all that,' he told himself.

He followed the direction the groom had pointed out and came to an ancient wall.

It was built of the same bricks as the house, and in the centre of it there was an iron gate which was open and the Marquis walked through.

He became conscious of the scent of flowers and herbs, which seemed somehow different from any sensations he had ever experienced.

The beds were neatly arranged around the four walls and in the centre of the garden there was a fountain which was obviously very old. The bowl was carved with fish and birds, and in the centre a cupid held a large fish. The water from the fish was being flung high into the air to catch the sunlight.

It was a most attractive ornament and as Flora moved towards him from behind it, he thought that she looked like a nymph who might have risen from the pool in which Narcissus had been drowned.

Flora was obviously surprised to see him.

He had to admit that she looked very lovely. She was carrying a basket of flowers and leaves and wearing a green dress which reminded him that it was Spring.

When she saw the expression on the Marquis's face she exclaimed,

"What has – happened! What is – wrong?"

The Marquis had anticipated she would know instinctively that something had happened.

"I do not expect that anyone will be very upset," he answered, "but Potter is dead."

"Dead! But how?"

"He shot himself," the Marquis replied. "He must have discovered that, as I had returned unexpectedly, it was impossible for him to cover up his crimes."

"Perhaps this will make things easier," Flora murmured as if she was speaking to herself.

"That is what I thought," the Marquis agreed. "I have sent for a doctor and I think the best move I could now make is to see the Chief Constable. Have you any idea who he is now?"

"Of course I have," Flora answered. "He is Sir Richard Carson, a very nice, helpful man and he lives about two miles away."

She paused for a moment before she added, "I remember him saying that he had not yet met you."

"I recall hearing about two years ago that the old Chief Constable, who was a friend of my father's, had died when he was nearly ninety."

"You must go and see Sir Richard at once." Flora urged, "so I will come to the castle a little later. Perhaps directly after luncheon would be best."

"I shall hope to be back by then, and I can only beg the new Chief Constable to keep what has happened here as quiet as possible."

"I am sure he will do so if you ask him," Flora said.

The Marquis looked round.

"So this is your herb garden."

"It has been here ever since the house was built," Flora replied, "and I think everyone who has owned it has been called locally a *White Witch*."

"And you say that is what they call you too?" the Marquis asked and there was a slightly sarcastic note in his voice.

He believed she was being somewhat dramatic about her position.

"All I try to do," Flora said quietly, "is to heal people of their ailments as Mother Nature intended that they should be healed."

"By herbs?"

"Of course," she answered. "If you think about it, or rather read about it, you will find that nature always adjusts herself to whatever is necessary. Nothing in nature is ever wasted."

The Marquis frowned a little as if he was trying to follow what she was saying.

"I know you think that is a lot of Fairy Tales," she said, "but you have to admit that trees eventually become coal and, if there is an excess of anything which might be too abundant, nature somehow disposes of it or controls it."

The Marquis did not want to agree with her. He remembered that when he was in Scotland and there were too many grouse on his estate, they contracted grouse disease. He had also heard that an excess of stags meant that many died for lack of food.

"I suppose you are right," he agreed a little reluctantly. "But if I am ill, I think I would still rather trust a doctor."

"That is what your grandmother did," Flora asserted, "and he could do nothing for her rheumatism. But now she intends to get up tomorrow so that she can be with you."

"What have you given her?" the Marquis enquired warily.

"Dandelion, wallflower, horsetail, wintergreen, chickweed and comfrey."

She reeled off the names and when she noticed the Marquis's face she laughed.

"All right." she said, "you do not believe me. Then go and talk to your grandmother and I could bring you two or three dozen witnesses from the village if I cared to do so."

The Marquis held up his hands.

"Let me say I will try to believe you, Miss Flora, but I find it difficult to connect dandelion and chickweed with magic."

Flora just smiled as he said,

"I must be on my way to the Chief Constable and will look forward to seeing you at about two o'clock."

"I will try not to keep your Lordship waiting." Flora replied.

The Marquis turned away and as he left the herb garden, he had a distinct feeling that she was laughing at him.

'Really she must think I am a fool,' he told himself, 'to believe that chickweed and all that other load of rubbish could cure rheumatism!'

He was convincing himself that it was because his grandmother was resting and enjoying the fresh country air at the castle that she was feeling so much better.

Doubtless the food Mrs. Bowles was cooking for her was fresher than anything she would be able to buy in London.

As he rode cross country towards the Chief Constable's house, he was wondering how he could persuade Flora how mistaken she was in her belief in herbs.

At the same time he was planning how he could escape from Locadi.

'If she does not see me,' he muttered to himself, 'she will doubtless take another lover and forget all about me.'

But he could sense that this was just wishful thinking. Where else would she find a man of his position and wealth and who was free to marry her?

Most of the Marquis's contemporaries had married when they were quite young. Their wives were chosen for them in the same way that Royalty arranged the marriages of their children.

The Marquis's father had of course tried to choose a bride for him before he was twenty-one.

For the first time in his life the Marquis, or rather the

Earl as he had been then, had been brave enough to defy his father. He declared that he had no intention of marrying someone whom he hardly knew and with whom he was not in love.

He had been able to take this strong attitude because his Godmother had recently died leaving him enough money to keep him independent of his parsimonious father, who had kept Ivor, his only son, extremely short of money.

Ivor's pocket-money had been smaller than that of any of his contemporaries at Eton and Oxford and he had not been able to afford the luxuries that all the other students of any social standing enjoyed.

When his mother died, his father's behaviour towards him had been even more unpleasant than before.

He had always resented his son and had always done everything he could to crush his will and prevent him from asserting himself.

So with his own money, Ivor found a freedom that he had never known in his life and because he could now afford it, he had started to travel.

It was one way of avoiding his father and the continual heckling he was forced to endure from him.

He had found it absorbing to travel first to France and Italy and then to visit Egypt, Constantinople and of course Greece.

The Marquis had always been an avid reader because he was allowed few companions and when at home he found he could escape from listening to his disagreeable father by being absorbed in one of the many books which filled the large library. They had been collected over the centuries although the fourth Marquis had contributed very little towards them.

One of the Marquis's first actions on inheriting the title was to restock the library. He had bought a great number of famous books published in his father's lifetime which had been ignored.

*

When the Marquis reached the Chief Constable's house, he was relieved to find Sir Richard was at home and surprised but delighted to meet him.

"I had no idea you had returned, my Lord," he said, "and it is very kind of you to call on me so quickly."

"I wish I could say it was for a happier reason than the one which brings me here," the Marquis replied.

He told the Chief Constable about the tragedy he had discovered and how horrified he was to learn of Potter's behaviour whilst he had been abroad.

"I did hear that matters were difficult on your estate and in the village," the Chief Constable remarked, "but I was told it was on your orders and felt it was not within my powers to interfere."

"I only wish that someone had let me know what was happening," the Marquis observed. "I can assure you that I would have come home immediately."

Once again he felt guilty that he had been persuaded by Locadi to stay so long in London after he had returned to England.

"I am sure that now, my Lord, you will put things to rights," the Chief Constable said, "and if I can help you in any way, I am happy to do so."

"Thank you," the Marquis said. "In the first place, I would be grateful if this most unpleasant suicide could be kept as quiet as possible and not blown up in the local newspapers."

"I think that can be managed," the Chief Constable replied. "I know the owner of the County newspaper and I am sure he will do what I ask on your behalf."

"That is most kind and understanding of you."

The Chief Constable asked him to stay for luncheon, but he said he had an appointment with Miss Romilly.

Sir Richard's eyes seemed to light up.

"A charming young woman," he enthused, "and she has done a great deal of good. Her father, as I expect you know, is an extremely distinguished writer."

"He is too busy to see me at the moment," the Marquis said, "but I am hoping to renew his acquaintance when his book is finished."

"I cannot believe, my Lord, that there are many people who would find a book more important than yourself! But one always lives and learns."

The Marquis agreed and as Sir Richard walked with him to the door he said,

"I would be grateful if you would let me know what is happening in your village. I like to keep my eye on events as they occur in the County."

"What Miss Romilly is determined I should do at the moment," the Marquis said. "is to give a party and build a school. Until that is completed, the children will have to be taught in a room in the castle as there is nowhere else available."

The Chief Constable looked at him in surprise.

"I cannot believe it!" he exclaimed. "I have always been told how your father would never permit any meeting to be held in the castle and normally discouraged his neighbours from visiting him except on special occasions."

"That is true," the Marquis agreed. "but now I have returned I am determined that everything shall be different, so I have to make a start with a school in the castle."

"I can see Flora Romilly's hand in all this," the Chief Constable chuckled. "No wonder they call her the *White Witch*."

As the Marquis rode away he thought that once again he was back to witchcraft and it was a subject that made him shudder.

He still harboured a strong feeling that Locadi was menacing him, in fact stalking him like a tigress stalking its prey.

'What *can* I do?' he asked.

He thought that if the Vicar had been in residence he might have turned to him.

He was well aware that in Jamaica, which he had often visited, a newly built house was always exorcised as the inhabitants were invariably afraid that ghosts or other supernatural beings might have settled in.

He was quite certain that the Vicar of a small country parish would have no idea of the right service for such an occasion, nor would he believe it was necessary.

There were, as far as he was concerned, no ghosts at the castle and he had never seen nor heard of one.

There had been of course servants who had complained that they were frightened at night, especially in or around the Norman Tower. If they heard noises, the Marquis was quite certain that it was bats.

If they saw dark figures it was doubtless a stable boy waiting to pounce on a pretty girl when she came out of the back door.

What he was dealing with, where Locadi was concerned, was very different indeed.

He did not suppose that any of Flora's herbs would be a viable antidote that could prevent Locadi forcing him to think of her.

Nor would they stop her from being perpetually in his dreams.

He arrived back at the castle just a few minutes before it was time for luncheon and again Mrs. Bowles had produced a delicious meal.

It was only when he was drinking his coffee and was told that Miss Flora had arrived that he felt guilty. For the first time it struck him that he might have invited her to luncheon.

He certainly did not want to emulate his father who disliked people coming into the castle and kept them away if he possibly could.

Equally as he had surmised earlier, he had no wish to encourage this girl to be aware of him as a man.

He would have been very stupid indeed if he had not known how easy it was for women to be attracted to him, not just on account of his title but because he was extremely good-looking.

Locadi was not the only beauty who had stalked him and there were indeed a number of others to whom he had succumbed or had avoided because they had not attracted him.

He understood, without being conceited, what happened when he entered a ballroom. A great number of women would look at him as if they were longing for him to be aware of their attractions.

Since he was twenty years old the *debutantes* of families of equal standing to his own had been paraded before him like foals at a Newmarket Spring sale.

'For the moment,' the Marquis told himself, 'I have finished with women completely and utterly. Locadi has shown me how dangerous they can be, and I am not such a fool as to need to learn the same lesson twice!'

He was however very conscious of the fact that he was not yet rid of Locadi – she would not easily give up the chase.

She also possessed a weapon against which, at the moment, he could muster no defence.

'I will not think about her. I will keep her out of my thoughts and out of my life!' He almost spoke the words aloud.

As he walked out of the dining room, he had the uncomfortable feeling that he heard her laugh!

Flora was waiting for him in the attractive blue drawing room which was used when there were only a few people in the house.

The curtains and covers were blue and over the mantelpiece hung a magnificent portrait. It was of the third Earl as a boy, dressed in a blue satin suit. It was especially prized by the family, and the Marquis had loved it ever since he had been small.

He remembered asking his mother if he could wear a blue suit too.

She had smiled as she replied,

"You will be laughed at, darling, if you wear a satin suit like that at your age. But if I can persuade your father to give you a fancy dress party at Christmas, then you shall have one."

The Marquis had looked forward to it, but his father had refused to entertain the idea and the party had never taken place.

Now as he entered the room he saw Flora looking up at the blue boy.

She was such an attractive sight as she stood there.

It passed through the Marquis's mind that most women when they were waiting for him watched the door as they were not interested in anything else.

"I see you are admiring the blue boy," he declared as he walked towards her.

"He is so beautifully painted," she answered, "and I am always sorry that when he grew up he had an exceedingly unhappy marriage."

"So you know about that."

"Of course," she answered. "I have read your family history. It would have been very strange to live next door and not be interested in all the fascinating accomplishments of the Wyns over the centuries."

"I suppose I should be gratified that you have taken so much interest in us," the Marquis remarked.

"I was an only child, as you were," Flora replied, "and I therefore made companions of the children I read about in books and the blue boy was one of them."

"So you too found it lonely to be an only child, but I am sure your home was a happy one."

"Very happy. Yet because my father and mother were so absorbed in each other, I often felt a little unwanted and that was when I would retreat into the garden or the woods."

She did not need to say any more as the Marquis knew exactly what she meant.

She had believed that there were elves digging under the trees. There were nymphs in the pools, and the red squirrels and the rabbits were her companions because she had no one else.

Before he could speak Flora looked at him and said,

"So you did the same?"

She was reading his thoughts again and the Marquis could not lie.

"I was exceedingly unhappy after my mother died, and in the holidays the horses, the dogs and of course the woods made up for the lack of boys of my own age."

He felt as he spoke that he was being too familiar with someone he hardly knew.

But Flora replied,

"I know exactly what you felt and if I ever marry I shall have a very large family so that none of them will ever feel lonely."

"What do you mean, if you ever marry?" the Marquis enquired. "Surely it is something you should be thinking of doing right now."

Flora shook her head.

"I have no intention of marrying anyone until I really fall in love, and I mean the love that I have read so much about and which is very different from what I see happening around me."

The Marquis understood that she was expressing her innermost thoughts without really thinking of who was listening to her.

"You surprise me," he said after a moment's pause. "I have always believed that young women like yourself start looking for the most important suitor and are determined to marry him, almost as soon as they have left the schoolroom."

Flora laughed.

"You are thinking about the *debutantes* in London," she said. "I have heard how the poor little things are just pushed up the aisle, having no idea of the difficulties of marriage or how they should handle a husband."

"And you, of course, know all about it," the Marquis said sarcastically.

He felt sure that she was only showing off, but Flora answered him quite seriously.

"I have coped with dozens of matrimonial problems in this village and the villages around us. The girls come to me asking for a talisman which will make a man propose, or asking how they can capture one who is already looking in a different direction."

She sighed before she continued,

"Then after their marriages they encounter further problems and because I can give them useful herbs, they expect me to give them my advice as well and they try to do exactly what I tell them to do."

The Marquis could only stare at her. Eventually he asked her,

"How old are you?"

"I was always told that is a rude question," Flora retorted, "but if you are really interested, I shall be twenty-one next birthday."

"Then it is certainly high time you were married and starting to produce the large family you are planning."

Flora laughed.

"As I have no one to organise me," she said, "I can only be thankful that I am not being pushed up the aisle with some man who is eligible because he has money and is doubtless ambitious to be top of his profession."

She was speaking so scathingly that the Marquis could only smile.

"You certainly do surprise me, Miss Flora, and now you have the task of persuading me – and I must say rather against my will – to open the school for which I suppose we shall also have to find teachers."

Flora looked at him with a twinkle in her blue eyes.

"I have one good teacher already and two others in view, but of course, my Lord, they have to be paid and that, I can tell you, is something magic cannot do."

As they left the blue drawing room to decide on the room that Flora required for the pupils, the Marquis was laughing.

CHAPTER FOUR

The Marquis spent another restless night.

When he awoke he wondered how long he would continue to be so vividly aware of Locadi and to see her in his dreams no less vividly.

The more he thought about her, the more he realised she was a very determined and shrewd woman in addition to the fact that she undoubtedly practiced witchcraft.

She had made up her mind to marry him and he would have to be very astute to escape the trap she was setting for him.

Once again he wished he was in the East where he could consult a Priest, a Fakir or a Shaman about his predicament.

He was quite sure that if he consulted any of his friends in London they would simply laugh at him, adding that he had undoubtedly been drinking too much.

He had however travelled enough to know that his apprehension was far from being just an illusion. Magic was something that was practiced in every Eastern country.

He had been impressed yesterday when Flora showed him the room she had found in the castle that could serve as a temporary school.

It was in fact the old squash racquet court which the Marquis had forgotten even existed. It had been built by an earlier owner of the castle and was then restored for his father when he was a boy, but allowed to fall into disrepair when he himself had not used it. The problem had been that he knew no one to play with.

When Flora showed him the court attached to the East wing, he realised immediately that it would make an excellent schoolroom as it would not interfere in any way with the more precious parts of the castle.

There was a door on the side of the house by which the children could enter and there was actually a place where they could wash their hands and hang up their coats.

"It is very clever of you, Miss Flora, to have found the squash court," he said. "I had almost forgotten it existed."

"I am going to beg you, my Lord, to let us have some curtains for the windows. I have already spoken to Mrs. Shepherd, who says she has exactly the right curtains put away in one of the attics."

The Marquis smiled.

"I will leave it in your very capable hands, Miss Flora," he said, "and I can only hope that your protégés will not be too noisy."

"I am sure they will respect whatever you ask of them," Flora said, "and as I have told you I have found two more teachers."

She looked at him anxiously as she spoke.

He guessed that she was still worrying whether he would think so many teachers were too much of an expense.

He had written a letter to the Vicar last night asking him to return to the village and had tempted him with the offer of a very much increased stipend, in fact larger than he had indicated to Flora.

'It is just a question of money,' he told himself cynically as he sealed the envelope. He thought the same now when Flora was worrying whether he could afford three teachers or not.

He guessed that she was speaking cautiously because she was quite determined that he should give a big party.

When he thought it over it seemed rather unnecessary.

At the same time if it would help to wash away the unpleasantness that had been created between the castle and the village, then it would certainly be worthwhile.

He thought that Potter's death might convince them that he had behaved extraordinarily badly and they would appreciate that his tales of his Master's meanness were nothing but lies.

Equally a great number of people had suffered acutely and it would undoubtedly take them a long time to forget their hardship.

The Marquis was determined today to call on his tenant farmers, but he then realised to his annoyance that he did not know their names.

He felt it would be a mistake to ask Gower or any of the senior servants as they would expect him to know the names himself.

He knew that the names must be written in the account books that Potter kept in his office, but the police were still going in and out. They were preparing to remove the body and it was not the moment for him to make an appearance.

*

Therefore once again he felt the need to ride to the *Four Gables* to find Flora. When he reached the house, the groom told him as before that Miss Flora was to found in the herb garden.

The Marquis wondered why she should spend so much time there when she should be concentrating on more important matters.

When he walked through the main gate of the herb garden he found that she was not alone. There were three children with her, two little girls and a small boy.

She did not see the Marquis at first.

He observed that she was showing the children different herbs and telling them what illnesses they could cure.

He thought this was a great waste of time and walked down the narrow path towards Flora in an almost indignant manner.

She now heard him coming and looked up.

Then she whispered to the children so that when he reached them the little girls curtsied and the small boy bowed.

"You are early, my Lord," she greeted him, "I thought you would be out riding."

"I am going a little later," the Marquis replied, "in fact I am on my way but I would like to talk to you first."

The way he spoke made it obvious that he wanted to speak to her alone.

"I tell you what you can do," Flora said to the children. "You can go to the house and ask Mrs. Brownlow, whom you know, to give you some milk to drink and some of her gingerbread biscuits to eat."

The small boy made a whoop of joy,

"I likes those gingerbread biscuits, miss, they're scrumptious!"

"I am sure Johnny, she could spare you two or three," Flora suggested, "so hurry to the house and I will come and find you as soon as I can."

"You'll not forget, Miss Flora," one of the girls piped up, "that Mama wants some of your cream for the burn on her hand."

"I will have it all ready for you to take home with you when you leave," Flora promised.

"Mama said I was to thank you very much," the child said.

"You can thank me when you receive it."

The two little girls ran down the path hand in hand, but Johnny stayed behind for a moment.

"You've not given me anything, Miss Flora, for the cut on my hand! It hurts when I touches it."

"I have something prepared for you in the house and you shall not leave without it."

He smiled at her and ran after the two girls.

Flora looked up at the Marquis as if to ask, 'and now what do *you* want?'

"Are you really teaching those small children to understand herbs?" he asked. "Surely it is a waste of your time."

"I think they enjoy listening to whatever I have to tell them," Flora answered, "and I am sure, although you will not believe me, that this knowledge will help them all through their lives."

The Marquis thought that this was an absurd exaggeration but it would be rude of him to say so.

Instead he said,

"I have come to *see* you because I have forgotten the names of my tenant farmers, and it is not convenient for me at the moment to examine the ledgers at Potter's house."

"I can understand *that*," Flora said, "and of course I will give the names to you. We will have to go back to the house so that I can write them down."

They walked towards the gate and then on an impulse the Marquis said,

"You talk so much about the good that herbs can do,

72

but what about the bad ones which are often used in the East to harm or kill an enemy."

"I suppose that does happen," Flora responded quietly. "Mine is the white magic in which we all want to believe, but there is also black magic."

"And what are the evil herbs called?" the Marquis asked.

Flora did not speak for a moment as if she was thinking and then she said,

"I suppose the most ancient of those plants is the mandrake. But it can be both good and bad. In fact the mystics called it the *love-hate* plant."

"What do you mean by that?" the Marquis asked.

"The mandrake is used in black magic and at the same time it is endowed with mysterious powers against demonic procession."

The Marquis drew in his breath. In a few sentences he had learnt, so he believed, exactly what he wanted to know.

If the mandrake would prevent Locadi from inflicting demonic possession on him, then he must possess the mandrake.

"I should like to see a mandrake," he said aloud, "because to be honest I have no idea what one would look like."

"I think most people would say the same, as the mandrake is shrouded in dark mystery and the supernatural."

"You must tell me more about it."

"Why are you suddenly so interested?" Flora asked. "I thought you did *not* approve of herbs."

"Now you are making things up. I do not disapprove, I only rather doubt that they are as effective as some people believe. As I have already told you that I prefer if I am ill to consult a doctor."

"Which of course I hope you never will be, but it would be a great triumph if the doctor failed and I succeeded in making you well again, as I have done with your grandmother."

"I was thinking before I came here," the Marquis said, "that it was really the fresh air and Mrs. Bowles's good food. Anyway we were talking about the mandrake, so please tell me all about it."

"It was originally Greek," Flora started, "and was known as the *Plant of Circe*, who used it in the magic brews by which she turned men into swine."

The Marquis gave an exclamation.

"I suppose I remember learning that when I read my first books on Greece, but I had no idea it was the mandrake that she used."

"It was certainly very effective," Flora asserted "but you should read what Papa quoted about it in one of his books."

"What is that?" the Marquis enquired.

"It was said, and these are the exact words, as near as I can remember them, '*never or very seldom to be found growing naturally, but under a gallows where the matter that hath fallen from the dead body hath given its root the shape of a man, the head of a woman and the substance of a female plant*'."

"It certainly sounds most unpleasant," the Marquis commented dryly.

"It is also recommended that the mandrake should be dug up at midnight if it is to be *really* effective."

By this time they had left the herb garden and were walking across the lawn.

The Marquis was wondering, if the mandrake was as effective as Flora believed it to be, where could he find such a plant?

He had the idea that she would not have permitted it to grow in her garden, even though it could help people like himself who were threatened by diabolical black magic.

Because he was afraid she would read his thoughts, he quickly talked about something else.

When they reached the house Flora wrote a list of the names of the farmers on the various farms he owned.

As the Marquis took the list from her he was still ruminating about the mandrake.

Without really considering the question he suggested,

"As you obviously know these people better than I do, why do you not come with me?"

Flora looked at him in surprise.

"Do you really want me?" she asked.

"I think you might be very useful," the Marquis replied.

There was a hint of laughter in the way he spoke as he thought she was fishing for a compliment and he was not prepared to give it to her.

However she answered him seriously,

"If that is true, then of course I am willing to come and help you make amends for the disgraceful way they have been treated by Potter."

She looked at the clock and added,

"You will have to give me five minutes to change into my riding habit, and will you be kind enough to tell the groom who is holding your horse to saddle Sunshine for me?"

The Marquis felt that in a way he was being made use of but still obeyed.

Then sooner than he expected Flora came running

down the stairs and out through the front door to where her horse had been brought to join his.

"I left a message for Papa, saying that I might be away for some time," she told him.

The Marquis lifted her into the saddle.

"I suppose," she continued, "you appreciate that we may have to go hungry or eat luncheon at an Inn, where I can assure you they serve delicious bread and cheese if nothing else."

The Marquis laughed,

"I think I might be able to endure that for one day. At the same time it would be more pleasant to return to the castle."

Flora did not say anything more as they rode off.

The Marquis thought, although he was reluctant to admit it, that it was nice to have a companion on what was likely to be a long ride to the far corners of his estate.

*

By the time they had visited three farms, it was already one o'clock and Flora said she was feeling hungry.

They were a long way from the castle and there were two more farms for them to visit, not far from where they were at the moment.

The Marquis looked at his watch and as he put it back into his waistcoat pocket, he said,

"Very well, you win. Now where is this ancient Inn that serves such excellent bread and cheese?"

"If the bread is stale and the cheese is sour," Flora replied, "I shall be prepared to apologise but the place I was thinking of is only about half a mile from here."

"Good, please lead the way."

It did not take them long to travel the short distance.

When the Marquis saw the Inn, it was just as he had

expected. Black and white, very old and named the *Dog and Duck*.

The proprietor, an elderly man who was going bald, was overcome at seeing the Marquis.

"Tis a real honour, my Lord," he said. "I hears as how you had returned from abroad and I never expected you'd be a calling here."

"We are both very hungry." the Marquis declared, "so you must give us anything you have ready and we would like to be served sitting outside in the sunshine."

"Of course, my Lord," the proprietor said. "and the Missus'll do her best, but ye can't expect miracles when things have been real hard."

He did not wait for the Marquis to ask what the hardship had been, but carried on,

"If them farmers aren't given seed they'll have no crops, and if they've no crops they've no money to spend with me."

The Marquis knew that there could no argument against this logic, so he merely said, "everything is being changed since my return home and that is why I am calling on all the farms."

The old man looked at him suspiciously as if he thought he might be lying, before saying,

"If that be the truth, then God bless your Lordship."

"I promise you that it is," the Marquis replied, "and in the meantime, until things improve, I will remit your rent and in six months time we can talk about it again."

The landlord of the *Dog and Duck* stared at him as if he could not understand what he was hearing.

Then he ran into the kitchen shouting for his wife, bringing her back with him in a few seconds.

As she curtsied to the Marquis he told her what he had

been promised.

"I just don't believe it," the woman quivered, as the tears ran down her cheeks.

"You've saved us," she cried, "I were thinking we might have to go to the workhouse."

"There will be nothing like that." the Marquis affirmed, "and now as Miss Romilly and I are very hungry we would like you to bring us some food as quickly as possible. And some of your home brewed cider to drink."

The tears were still running down her cheeks as the proprietor's wife disappeared into the kitchen.

The Marquis drew Flora outside.

There was a long wooden seat with a table in front of it from which they could see the whole of the green with the duck-pond at the end of it.

"You have made two people very happy," Flora said quietly.

"How could anyone guess that one man could cause so much trouble and distress?" the Marquis asked.

"I know it is difficult for you to understand, but it was terrible for Papa and me to watch all this happening and know that there was only so little we could do to help those who were around us."

"I suppose what has occurred here has happened in a dozen or so other places," the Marquis said angrily.

"I think you will find some are worse and some are better, but now that everything has changed they will think of you as a saviour and a hero and not as a greedy monster, or rather a dragon gobbling them all up!"

"Now you are frightening me," the Marquis said, "and I am afraid that I shall not be able to go abroad again without fearing that this sort of chaos will happen once more in my absence."

"You will just have to be more careful who you leave in charge," Flora suggested.

She gave a little sigh before she added,

"I suppose there are greedy men to be found everywhere in the world and of course it all comes back to what St. Paul said, *'love of money is the root of all evil'*."

"But life can be very uncomfortable without money," the Marquis remarked dryly.

There was a short silence before Flora enquired,

"Do you ever wish that you were an ordinary man?"

The Marquis looked at her in surprise.

"What do you mean by that?"

"Exactly what I say. You are a Marquis, you are rich, you own a great deal of property, possess the best horses and people are of course very respectful to you."

"Some are even exceptionally pleasant."

"Yes, but how would you manage if you had none of these advantages and were just a man finding the world an adventure rather than a bed of roses?"

It was a question that the Marquis had never been asked before, nor for that matter had he really thought about it.

"I suppose," he said slowly, "I should strive to better myself, in fact to become what I am now."

Flora gave a little laugh.

"Then you are very lucky, most people would want much more than that."

"Much more? What do you mean by that?"

"I think there are many people who want to touch the stars and are not content with just the humdrum material things of life. No matter how comfortable they are, they still yearn for something more."

"And what stars do you wish to touch?" the Marquis asked her quizzically.

"I think really that I just want to help people who cannot help themselves. The children to start with and those who grow up but are still childlike and incapable of coping with the world as it is."

"That sounds a commendable aim," the Marquis observed. "Equally as I have told you already, you should be thinking of getting married, having a family and bringing them up to be good citizens."

"I am quite prepared to do all that when the time comes," Flora answered. "But I shall still want more. It is not my heart and my body that is hungry but my brain."

The Marquis knew exactly what she was saying. In a way it was what he had always wanted for himself.

It was something more than just living in the world as it is and that need was what he had sought in his travels.

When he had explored the Pyramids in Egypt, the Himalayas in Nepal and Delphi in Greece, he had felt they had secrets to tell him.

Flora was watching the expression in his eyes and suddenly she exclaimed,

"You do understand! How extraordinary! I never thought you would!"

"Why should you think that I was so stupid, or perhaps the word should be unimaginative."

Flora put her elbows on the table and rested her chin in her hands.

"I think perhaps I was still hating you as I did when you were abroad. People came to see Papa and me because they were desperate and had no idea where they could go for help."

"And you helped them."

"As best we could, but we are not rich like you. What the majority of them really needed was money as well as sympathy and understanding."

"You can hardly do that for the whole world."

"Of course not," Flora agreed, "but we can at least try. That is why Papa's books are important because he makes people think."

"I suppose I have been very remiss in not asking what he is writing about at the moment. I remember reading one of his books a long time ago and being most impressed with it."

"What Papa is writing now is his theory on the influence of religion on civilisation, going back to the very beginning when men consulted witch doctors because there was no one else."

The Marquis thought that inevitably they were moving back to magic, which was a subject he did not wish to discuss with Flora in case she should read his thoughts.

He was therefore relieved when their lunch was brought to the table.

They had already been sipping an excellent home-brewed cider, but now the well-cooked meal the proprietor's wife had brought them was even more delicious because they were both so hungry.

The Marquis certainly ate everything that was on offer and when they had finished he announced,

"I have enjoyed this luncheon more than any meal I have eaten since I returned home."

Even as he said it, because it was true, he sensed that once again Locadi was nearby.

He could feel her almost as if she was standing beside him and when he looked across the green, he could see her eyes.

He pushed his plate away from him abruptly,

"I think we should be on our way, I have no wish to be too late returning home."

The tone of his voice was very different to the way he had been speaking previously.

Flora looked at him in surprise and as he rose from the table and walked without speaking to where they had stabled their horses, she realised that something was wrong.

She wondered at first if it was something that she had said or done, but her instinct told her it was much worse.

She could not imagine what was troubling the Marquis, but undoubtedly it was very real and she wanted to help.

He was so very different from what she had expected.

She had observed from the way he talked to the farmers they met that he was exactly the right Master they should have.

She knew now that she could trust him. In fact all the unkind things she had thought about him in his absence were unjustified. He was exactly what the owner of the castle should be, she told herself.

She was aware that his kindness and understanding was something that came from his heart. It was not merely appropriate to the situation, which after all was none of his making.

'What is wrong now?' Flora asked herself. 'What can be troubling him?'

A man who was employed in the Inn brought their horses round to the front and the Marquis paid for their luncheon.

From the profuse thanks of the proprietor, it was obvious that he had been very generous.

When they rode off Flora was leading the way to

another farm that was about two miles distance, while the Marquis remained silent.

She glanced at him once or twice and when he did still not speak she finally asked him,

"What is wrong? Is it anything I have said or done?"

"No, of course not." the Marquis answered quickly.

"But you must admit there is something that is upsetting you?"

He did not answer for a moment because he did not wish to lie, before replying,

"It is nothing that you can deal with. It is a battle I need to fight myself."

"Let me help you."

The Marquis shook his head.

"I do not want to talk about it," he said. "Now tell me about the farmer we are now about to visit."

Flora did as she was told.

Then after they had visited him and one more farmer, they turned for home.

The Marquis left each farm with the farmer thanking him profusely.

He promised them that he would help with new buildings and provide them with new stock or whatever was needed in the fields.

As they rode towards the castle, Flora said,

"I am afraid it has been a very expensive day for you. I have lost count of how much you have promised to give away."

"The money is of no consequence. What is so appalling is that they should all have suffered almost to the point of despair just through the greed of one crooked man."

"Everything will be different now," Flora said, "and I

think perhaps when you look back you will find this has also been a turning point in *your* life."

"Why should you say that?" the Marquis asked sharply.

"You admit that you had no intention of coming here when you returned from abroad. Yet somehow and for some reason I do not know, you were guided back because you were needed here at this particular moment."

The Marquis thought it was not a question of guidance. It was more likely running away from something he could not control and of which, to be honest, he was becoming even more afraid.

"Whatever it was and if it still exists," Flora said in her soft voice, "you will find it easier to control the situation because of what you have achieved here."

"You mean that my people are now with me rather than against me?"

"Yes, of course. All of us when we are in trouble, need the love and support of those who believe in us and who can make us capable of great deeds."

The Marquis glanced at her and smiled. "You make it sound too easy," he said. "Life is much more difficult than that and having climbed one mountain, one always finds there is another much higher just ahead."

"It may be hard, but you can still reach the top," Flora responded with a voice of conviction which was rather moving.

"Can you be sure of that?" the Marquis asked.

"I am surer now than I have ever been before. I do not know what has been upsetting you, but I can feel that it is something dark and menacing which is trying to envelop you."

The Marquis found he was holding his breath.

"But you are strong enough," Flora resumed, "and

brave enough to win, however difficult it may seem."

She spoke very quietly.

The horses, as if they understood, gave no trouble and were moving slowly.

The Marquis was astounded.

He could not imagine how she could have any idea of what he was feeling or that he was afraid.

Yet she spoke as if he had asked for her advice and that she was giving him the right answer.

"I only hope that what you have told me will come true," he said quietly.

Then because he was afraid she might discover more than she knew already, he urged his horse ahead.

Both horses moved into a gallop.

A quarter of an hour later the castle was in sight.

The Marquis's mind was in a turmoil and he knew that he wanted to ask Flora for her help. Yet his common sense questioned what help could she possibly give him.

A few herbs growing in her garden would not have any effect on Locadi.

He had no wish to endure another restless night thinking of her, dreaming of her and waking only to think of her again.

He knew she was willing him with all her strength. She was pulling at him to make him return to London to be with her.

If he did so he was quite certain that by fair means or by black magic she would force him into marrying her.

'She must be demented to think that such a scheme is possible,' the Marquis told himself angrily.

At the same time he knew it was true. He was being haunted by a woman with whom he should never have become involved. Yet having been, he was now finding it almost impossible to escape her.

'What *can* I do? What the Devil can I do?' he asked as they rode on.

There was no answer and once again he was afraid that Flora would divine what he was thinking.

"It has been a most interesting and educational day," he managed to say in a cheerful tone.

"It has been a very productive time," Flora corrected him. "All the people you have spoken to have now been encouraged to do their best to bring their farm, the land and their animals back to the perfection you expect. I am quite certain that they will not fail you."

"You credit me with much greater powers than I aspire to possess," the Marquis said with a smile.

"I want you to touch the stars."

"Do you touch them?" he enquired.

"I try," she answered, "and just sometimes I succeed. I am always aware that they are there whenever I look up."

The Marquis thought she was the most unusual and original young woman he had ever met. In fact he could not remember any woman ever talking to him in such a manner.

And not, as they all did, trying to flirt with him.

Flora of course, as he knew, had hated and despised him before he returned. It was obviously difficult for her to change overnight and think of him as a handsome and attractive young man.

He accepted that.

Yet he found it hard to believe that any woman with whom he spent any length of time was more concerned with his behaviour to other people than to herself.

Not once during the day had Flora made any attempt to make him look at her as being an attractive woman.

He had the feeling that if he paid her the kind of compliments he paid Locadi, she would have been, if not shocked, at least a little uncomfortable.

He was sure now after all that she had said, she would be very disappointed if he failed her.

It was then that he worked out in his mind that she was thinking of him entirely as the owner of the castle and a great estate.

She expected him to behave, if not like one of the Gods, at least as a human and kindly potentate, looking after his people.

It was a position no woman had ever put him into before. While he found it intriguing, he was not certain that it was exactly a compliment.

In fact Flora wanted much from him that he could not give.

He felt he had to climb a mountain before she would ever be satisfied that he was doing everything that was required of him.

It was very different from what Locadi required. Once again as she came into his mind he felt himself shrinking from her nearness. He could see her eyes like those of the charm he had thrown into the river.

Once again she was hypnotising him into doing what she wanted.

'I have to be rid of her, I have to,' the Marquis thought frantically.

Because he felt somewhat desperate, he turned to Flora as if for protection.

"What have we to do when we reach the castle?" he asked her.

"We have a few more plans to make for the party," Flora replied, "and as the weather is so fine I think it would be a good idea to hold it on Saturday."

"Very well," the Marquis agreed, "if that is what you want."

"It is your party and it must be what you want," Flora answered.

The Marquis did not reply and she said,

"Please try to enjoy it. If you enjoy it, everyone else will too."

"I can hardly believe that I am suddenly so important to the people who have been abusing me and wishing I was dead."

"Already they have learnt that it was not your fault that Mr. Potter behaved in such an appalling manner. Now after all they have been through they want someone to love and look up to. But as I am sure you know, to receive love one has to give love."

"That is something I have never even considered," the Marquis admitted.

"Well, it is true. Because I love the children, they come to me with their rights and their wrongs, their happinesses and their unhappinesses."

She smiled at him before she continued,

"If you love your people, they will follow you because you are not only helping them, but inspiring them to do better."

The Marquis thought he had never participated in a more extraordinary conversation with any young woman.

By now they had reached the castle. They rode out of the fields and into the drive.

Now he could see the new stable-boys running round to the front of the house to wait for their horses.

"Thank you, Miss Flora," he said as they crossed the bridge over the lake. "It has been a very interesting day. I feel rather as if the school mistress has settled me down to a mathematical problem to which there is no easy solution."

Flora smiled.

"I am sorry. If I have been lecturing you, please forgive me. It is only because I know exactly what your people want and how much you can give them."

"You are quite certain that I can?"

"Quite certain," she answered.

The Marquis drew his horse to a standstill. He dismounted and then walked to Flora to lift her down.

She was very light and he felt she almost flew from the saddle to the ground without his help.

"Thank you," she said. "But you must be tired and perhaps I should go straight home."

"I know my grandmother would be very upset if she did not see you today. Also I think we have both earned a good cup of tea."

"I would certainly enjoy that," Flora agreed.

They walked up the steps and through the front door and as they entered the hall, Bowles announced,

"There is a lady to see you, my Lord."

The Marquis stood very still.

"A lady?" he questioned.

"Yes, my Lord. She arrived from London about an hour ago and said she thought you'd be expecting her."

For a moment the Marquis became speechless.

Then as if he thought it could not be true, he moved automatically across the hall.

A footman opened the door of the drawing room and he walked in.

Standing by the window looking extremely elegant but overdressed for the country was Locadi.

CHAPTER FIVE

It was with a considerable effort that the Marquis managed to force a smile to his lips.

"This is a great surprise, Locadi," he said, "I was not expecting you."

"As I did not hear from you, I felt sure you needed me," Locadi stated calmly, "and I missed you, I missed you terribly."

There was a throbbing note in her voice.

The Marquis turned hastily to Flora who had followed him into the room.

"Let me introduce, Miss Flora Romilly, who has been helping me to put things to rights on the estate, and we are now very busy arranging a village party to take place on Saturday."

He spoke as if it was impossible for Locadi to take any part in it.

"Then I hope dear, clever Ivor," she replied calmly, "that I may help you too. You know how much I admire you when you are organising things."

There was a silky sweetness in her voice which made the Marquis want to squirm. He disliked this conversation taking place in front of Flora and he wondered what she would think of him.

He looked to where an elaborate tea was laid out in front of the sofa.

"Will you pour the tea?" he said to Flora.

There was just a slight hesitation as if she thought he should have asked his new guest. Then obediently she sat down at the table and started to fill the tea cups from the George II silver teapot.

"A real English tea," Locadi said, "How exciting!"

She sat in an armchair which meant the Marquis had to carry her cup, saucer and plate to her. And to offer her the sandwiches and cakes which were on the tea-table.

"London has been very dull without you," she chattered. "Everyone asks when you are coming back, so I thought I would come and find out for myself."

"It was most kind of you," the Marquis said, "but I am afraid you will find it very dull here. Miss Flora and I are arranging a party for the villagers who have been badly treated by my estate manager whilst I have been away, and I think, Locadi, you would be far happier back amongst your friends in London."

"Not unless you come with me," Locadi replied.

She looked at him in a way which told the Marquis without further words that she had no intention of letting him escape.

He was wondering frantically what he could do when he remembered that his grandmother was upstairs.

Turning to Flora, he said,

"I hope that Grandmama is well enough to come down to dinner this evening."

"She has been longing to," Flora responded, "but I want her to rest as much as possible."

"As I have a guest tonight, I am sure she will be willing to chaperone us," the Marquis suggested.

He spoke as if he was joking and that a chaperone was quite unnecessary.

However Locadi frowned and he knew she was annoyed.

"What has been happening in London while I have been away?" he asked to change the subject.

"Nothing of any great consequence," Locadi replied, "except that of course I missed you at every ball and every reception."

She gave him a seductive glance as if she might have added, 'and every night as well.'

The Marquis quickly looked away.

Feeling that she was very much in the way, Flora drank her tea quickly and rose from the sofa.

"I must go upstairs and talk to her Ladyship," she told the Marquis. "I will tell her you expect her to come down to dinner, but she should not stay up too late."

"I understand," the Marquis replied.

As Flora walked towards the door, he hurried to open it for her.

Then as she stepped out into the passage he followed, closing the door behind him.

"Will you and your father do me a great favour and come here to dinner with me tonight," he asked in a low voice.

Flora looked surprised before answering,

"As it so happens we have the Chief Constable with Lady Carson and their son dining with us. Papa has practically finished his book and wants to celebrate."

For a moment the Marquis was silent before asking, "As they are coming to dinner with you and I would very much like to meet your father again, will you bring them to dine with me instead?"

Flora stared at him.

"I would be extremely grateful if you could arrange it," the Marquis urged.

There was an emphasis in his voice which Flora could not ignore.

"I suppose," she said slowly, "it could be managed. What time would you want us here?"

"The question is," the Marquis replied, "at what time have you asked your guests?"

"For dinner at eight o'clock."

"Then dinner at the castle will be at eight fifteen," he said, "and please do not fail me."

She looked up into his eyes and immediately understood that he was really pleading with her.

"I will not fail you," she breathed, "and I am sure that Papa will understand."

"I am very, very grateful, and now, as you are going up to see my grandmother, I will accompany you."

Flora was just about to ask what he was going to do with his new guest, when the Marquis moved a few steps into the hall and called to Bowles,

"Ask Mrs. Shepherd to look after Lady Marshall and to suggest that she rests before dinner as I have a great number of matters to attend to."

"I'll do that, my Lord."

The Marquis walked up the staircase beside Flora without speaking and when she knocked on the Dowager's bedroom door and walked in, he followed her.

"Oh, there you are, my dear," the Dowager greeted Flora. "You have been neglecting me."

"I have no wish to do that," Flora replied, "but the Marquis and I have covered a lot of ground today and helped a great number of people who are much happier this evening than they were this morning."

The Dowager smiled.

"I think they always feel like that when you have been with them, my dear."

The Marquis kissed his grandmother saying,

"I am going to ask you, Grandmama, to come down to dinner tonight because we have a party and of course you too must be present."

"It is something I am longing to do," she replied. "I am feeling so much better, thanks entirely to this dear child."

She patted Flora's hand as she said so and the Marquis said,

"Lady Marshall has arrived unexpectedly and of course we must entertain her."

"Lady Marshall!" the Dowager exclaimed. "I cannot imagine why you asked her to stay."

"Actually I did not ask her," the Marquis replied defensively, "she just walked in and I could hardly leave her sitting outside the front door."

He spoke with a hint of amusement in his voice, but Flora realised to her surprise that this was just the impression he wanted to portray.

"It sounds unlike her to arrive if the red carpet is not down and the band is not playing," the Dowager added sarcastically.

"That is why I felt I must give a party tonight," the Marquis said as if jumping at the excuse.

"Well, I would have been a great deal happier if I could have just been alone with you and Flora," the Dowager remarked.

"I have also asked Mr. Romilly," the Marquis continued, "and the Chief Constable and his wife."

"Oh, well, that is different. I shall enjoy meeting both

these distinguished gentlemen although I expect Lady Marshall will try to grab them before I can get a word in!"

"My money is on you, Grandmama."

She laughed and he bent to kiss her.

"Put on your best gown and all your diamonds and stun them!" he said. "You were a great beauty long before it was fashionable to become one."

The Dowager blushed and enjoyed the compliment.

Then when the Marquis had left the room, she said to Flora,

"Now what is all this about and why has Lady Marshall turned up unexpectedly?"

"She said she was missing his Lordship in London," Flora informed her frankly.

"I did hear he was seeing rather a lot of her," the Dowager replied, "and thought it was a mistake. She has a bad reputation and my friends have told me that now her husband is dead, she is looking for a rich bridegroom."

Flora looked at the Dowager in surprise.

She was thinking no one could be a more unsuitable chatelaine of Wyn Castle than the overdressed woman downstairs. There was no doubt she was beautiful, but there was something about her which was definitely unpleasant and in a way frightening.

Flora was not certain what it was, but she could feel it instinctively and she sensed that the Marquis was feeling the same.

'Surely she cannot harm him,' she thought apprehensively.

Yet her perception told her that here was an element of danger that she did not understand.

She talked to the Dowager for a little while longer and

then she slipped out of the house without seeing the Marquis and hurried home.

*

She needed to break the news to her father that they were dining at the castle and not at home. She also needed to persuade him that there was nothing wrong in taking their dinner-guests with them.

Fortunately her father was delighted at having completed his book, except for what he called 'the finishing touches'. He was therefore not really concerned about anything else.

"I suppose you are going to be busy with this party you are arranging at the castle," he had said. "So if I have a quiet day tomorrow and Saturday, I really think the manuscript can go to the publishers on Monday."

"That is wonderful news, Papa!" Flora cried. "I am sure they will be delighted. They have kept asking when the book will be ready."

"I do not believe they will be disappointed," her father replied, "I consider it the best and certainly the most informative book I have ever written.

Flora kissed him.

"You are so brilliant, Papa, and I know if Mama was with us she would be as thrilled as I am."

"You are a good girl, Flora," he said, "and it must have been very dull for you these past months while I have been so busy. But now we will make up for it, and we might even go to France for a short while."

"That will be lovely, Papa."

She knew as she spoke she did not really want to go away.

Now that the Marquis was back at the castle there was so much for him to do and he needed her help.

96

She had no wish to leave the village and she found this rather surprising considering that before the Marquis's return she had felt so depressed.

She had longed to get away from all the misery of the villagers if only for a few days.

Now everything was changed and she had enjoyed today more than she had enjoyed any day for a very long time.

It was sheer delight to see the farmers looking happy again.

Their faces had lit up when the Marquis told them what they could now do and that he would finance any sensible project they brought to him.

The farmer's wives had been moved to tears.

When they had ridden away, Flora felt that they looked younger than they had for over a year.

'He is doing exactly the right thing,' she told herself.

At the same time she could not help feeling that a great deal of it was due to her. He was in fact relying on her in a way that she found most flattering.

As her father had agreed to the changed arrangements for dinner, she hurried upstairs to decide what she would wear.

She had not worried much about her appearance when things were so difficult all around them. But now she became self-conscious of her somewhat neglected wardrobe.

She looked at her evening gowns and wondered which was the most attractive, but there was not a great deal of choice.

Finally she selected a gown of pale pink chiffon, which made her look very young and ethereal.

When the Marquis saw her, he was distinctly reminded of the buds that were bursting out on the fruit trees.

Back at the castle, the Marquis was deliberately making work for himself to try to take his mind off the vexed question of Locadi.

He was very angry that she should have followed him, but he told himself it was something he might have expected.

He understood exactly why she had come.

After the restless nights he had spent finding it impossible to escape from her image, he was now faced with the reality of her in person.

'What *shall* I do?' he asked himself again and again.

The question remained unanswered when finally he walked slowly upstairs for his bath and to dress for dinner.

He was determined if at all possible not to be left alone with Locadi. He was not only afraid of recriminations and reproaches, but also that she might entice him further into her clutches.

'If I could find an antidote to black magic,' he thought as he tied his evening tie, 'I would use it now'.

Once again he was reflecting on the mandrake, but where could he obtain one?

He deliberately waited until his grandmother was ready to descend the stairs, so that he could escort her down to dinner.

He suspected and found that he was right, that Locadi had gone down early hoping to talk to him alone. He had given her no chance to succeed, having the Dowager beside him.

Shortly after they reached the drawing room, the rest of the party arrived.

The Marquis was interested to see that Frederick Romilly was an extremely good-looking man and as he might have expected he had a delightful voice and a very distinctive way of talking.

"I must welcome you home, my Lord," he said to the Marquis. "My daughter has told me about the great deal you have to do, but of course it is better late than never."

"That is what I have been telling myself," the Marquis replied, "but the estate should not have fallen into such a disgraceful condition in the first place."

The Chief Constable was obviously delighted at his invitation to dinner at the castle and the Marquis found that Lady Carson was an attractive person with a sympathetic manner which he found most soothing.

It was definitely something he needed after seeing the expression in Locadi's eyes when he entered the room with his grandmother on his arm.

It was strange sensation, he thought, but now he no longer found her beautiful – in fact she was almost repulsive.

He did not understand how his feelings could have changed so quickly and he decided that it was primarily because she now scared him.

'It is ridiculous to be frightened of a woman,' he told himself.

Yet he discerned when he met Locadi's eyes that she was sending out waves towards him which it was difficult to repel or ignore.

They walked into the dining room.

The Marquis had arranged the table very astutely.

"Because it is your first night downstairs Grandmama," he announced, "you must sit on my right."

"I am delighted to be seated in the place of honour, dear boy," the Dowager answered.

It was then correct that Lady Carson should sit on his left.

He arranged the other guests so that Locadi was sitting

on the right of the Chief Constable, who was placed next to his grandmother.

Mr. Romilly was on her other side, leaving young Henry Carson, who was always known as Harry, to sit next to Flora.

The Marquis noticed how well they seemed to be getting on.

He felt that he should be pleased that Flora was taking his advice and finding an eligible young gentleman in the neighbourhood, yet he also decided very forcibly that he did not think Harry Carson was good enough for her.

He was in fact an extremely handsome young man of about twenty-three, who had come down from Oxford with a good degree and was determined to seek a position in the Foreign Office.

'She could do better than him,' the Marquis thought to himself.

Then he wondered why he should be worried or concerned about the love affairs of a local country girl.

The conversation however seemed to revolve around Flora.

"I hear," the Chief Constable said in an amused voice, "that you are actually opening a school in the castle. I think that must be a major triumph for which you should receive an award."

"It was not as difficult as it may sound," Flora answered, "and I have actually left his Lordship with the ball room, the music room, the library and the picture gallery all for himself!"

They laughed at her remark before the Dowager added,

"And of course you have left him the Chapel too. It seems a pity that it is not big enough for the children to say their prayers there each morning before they start their lessons."

"I had not thought of that," Flora admitted.

"You are so lucky to have a Chapel in the castle," Lady Carson said. "Our Church is over a mile from us, and it is always a nuisance having to send the older members of the household in one of our carriages as they cannot walk so far to Church."

"We are fortunate enough to boast two Chapels," the Dowager intervened.

"*Two*!" Lady Carson exclaimed. "How is that possible?"

"I see that being new to the County you have not heard of the Chapel in the shrubbery," the Dowager replied.

"How fascinating!" Lady Carson enthused. "Do tell us all about it."

"It was the sixth Earl who built it. After living a most outrageous and dissolute life, he repented of his sins in his old age. He was actually the last Earl, because his son became the first Marquis."

The Chief Constable laughed,

"I hope we do not all have to follow his example."

"Earl William repented very thoroughly," the Dowager continued. "He built himself a small hut where he slept and constructed a very beautiful Chapel right next to it."

"How extraordinary," Lady Carson exclaimed.

"His family still lived in the castle," the Dowager resumed, "but every night and most of the day he stayed in his little hut or knelt praying in the Chapel."

"What an amazing story!" Lady Carson said, "I would love to see the Chapel. Is it very dilapidated?"

"Not at all," the Dowager replied. "At least it was not a year ago. It has always been looked after by the head gardener's wife, and I believe, although I have not asked since I have been here this time, that she even puts flowers on the altar every week."

Flora knew exactly what the Dowager was saying as she had visited the Chapel in the shrubbery several times.

It had been designed by one of the finest architects of the time, who had concentrated on the carvings, the stained-glass windows and the very beautiful altar made from marble brought all the way from Italy.

"Do you ever hold a service there now?" Locadi asked the Marquis.

He shook his head.

"We have our larger Chapel here in the castle which can hold all the staff. They also go to the Parish Church, which is just at the end of the park on festive occasions."

He paused before he added,

"And of course the family all go to the larger Chapel to be buried."

"And also I suppose," Locadi said softly, "to be married?"

The Marquis pretended he had not heard the question.

He turned to ask Lady Carson some question about their horses and if her son was a good rider.

"We are all hoping that, because you own the best land for the occasion that you will arrange a point-to-point or a steeplechase," she replied. "Or is that too much to ask so soon?"

"Not at all," the Marquis answered. "I shall certainly consider your suggestion and I am sure it is something I would enjoy myself."

"And which you will undoubtedly win, my Lord," Harry Carson chipped in. "So you ought to be handicapped!"

"I will think about that," the Marquis responded, "but as I shall have to present the prizes, I will be forced to eliminate myself even if I am the winner!"

They were still talking about horses when dinner came to an end.

The Dowager rose saying to Lady Carson,

"I think the ladies should leave the gentlemen to their port and I hope they will not be too long before joining us."

"We will not keep you waiting, Grandmama," the Marquis volunteered.

The Dowager led the way back into the drawing room. Flora walked to the window.

She knew the Marquis had given orders that the fountain which was just outside the drawing room should be turned on and thought how lovely it would look in the moonlight.

She was not mistaken.

There was a full moon that night and the sky was filled with glittering stars. They were all reflected in the water being flung high into the air from the fountain.

It was much more impressive than the fountain in Flora's herb garden.

The spray from the fountain made her feel, as her own did, that the water was like prayers rising towards the sky, hoping to be heard.

Then suddenly a voice beside her said,

"Tell me, Miss Romilly, how long have you known the Marquis?"

It was Locadi who was speaking.

Flora knew instinctively that the question was somehow barbed.

As the older woman spoke Flora could feel vibrations of resentment and dislike coming from her.

"I have not known him for long, although my father knew his father," Flora replied. "But I have been able to help him a little in repairing some of the damage that was done whilst he was away abroad."

"I should have thought there were plenty of other people to do that for him," Locadi commented tartly.

Flora did not reply, and after a moment Locadi continued,

"Perhaps I should let you into a secret. His Lordship and I are engaged to be married, but I have been in mourning for the past year and it will look disloyal to my late husband if I married again too quickly."

"I understand and of course you have my good wishes."

"I will make it very clear," Locadi resumed, "that Ivor belongs to me, and therefore it would be a mistake for you to waste your time running after him."

There was a short spiteful tone in her voice and Flora stiffened.

"I hope," she said, "that I would never run after any man and certainly not one who is engaged to another woman."

"I am glad to hear that you are so sensible, but do not forget that what I have told you is a secret, and we must wait a little while before Ivor's family is told and of course mine. *Just leave Ivor alone.*"

She snarled as she turned away and walked back to the sofa to join the Dowager.

She sat down beside her and started to gush in an exaggerated fashion over the castle.

"It must have broken your heart," she said to the Dowager, "when your husband died and you had to leave here. I always think it is so sad that the widows of noblemen lose not only their husbands but their homes as well."

"I was so glad for my son to inherit the castle," the Dowager replied quietly, "and as I enjoy being in London I spend more time there than in the Dower House, which I find rather dull."

"Of course you do," Locadi agreed, "and because you are so beautiful, as your grandson has already told me, I am sure there are plenty of gentlemen in London to pay you compliments and of course escort you wherever you wish to go."

The Dowager made a brief response and started to talk to Lady Carson about the country.

A short while later the gentlemen returned to join the ladies.

The Marquis found Locadi sitting silently and looking sour.

Flora was at the window still watching the fountain.

He wanted to join her but knew it would be a mistake.

He remembered that when he was in London, Locadi was jealous of any woman he talked to whilst he was with her, and if he admired someone she immediately pulled them to pieces.

'It's absurd to think that she might be jealous of Flora,' he tried to tell himself.

At the same time he knew she would be resentful and in consequence very offensive. He therefore talked to Fredrick Romilly about his book.

It was still quite early when the Dowager announced that she thought she should go to bed.

"It is my first day up," she said, "and although I have enjoyed every minute of the evening, I am determined to be well enough to watch the fireworks on Saturday night."

"Are you having fireworks?" Lady Carson asked the Marquis. "Oh, please may I come? I do love fireworks and

105

I have only seen really good ones once or twice in my life?"

"And I would like to come too," Harry said. The Marquis laughed.

"The more the merrier. Of course you can all come. I shall be delighted to invite you all."

He turned to his grandmother.

"Incidentally," he said, "Gower tells me that in the coach-house he has found the boat that was lit up on my twenty-first birthday. Do you remember it?"

"Of course I do," the Dowager replied. "Can you use it again?"

"I have every intention of doing so," the Marquis said. "It shall be lit up for all the small boys who will think it is a fairy ship that will carry them to unknown parts of the world."

"Is that what you believed when you were young?" Flora asked.

"Yes funnily enough it was," the Marquis admitted.

"And that was why later you wanted to go exploring when you grew up," Flora remarked.

"I think really," he replied, "that it was a desire to get away from everything that made me unhappy, and also to see for myself the world outside my own estate."

Flora laughed.

"You certainly succeeded," she said. "Who could imagine that you could travel to so many exciting places which I have only read about in Papa's books."

"One day perhaps you will visit them yourself," the Marquis suggested.

Flora gave a sigh.

"I do hope so, but I expect it will just be in my dreams."

The Marquis thought that was what he would like to be

sure of dreaming tonight. Instead of which he forced his thoughts to a standstill.

He was suddenly afraid of what would happen when his guests left and he would be left alone with Locadi.

Mr. Romilly was already saying goodbye.

"It has been such a delightful evening," he said to the Marquis, "and I hope that you will dine with us one night soon."

"I shall be delighted," the Marquis replied.

The Chief Constable made a similar invitation and Lady Carson added,

"You will see us on Saturday. Are you quite certain you do not mind us all coming to watch the fireworks?"

"I am charmed that you should do so," the Marquis said, "and I hope they will not disappoint you."

"I am sure I shall be thrilled with them," Lady Carson answered.

The Marquis took them to the front door and escorted them into their carriages.

Then he gave his grandmother his arm and helped her up the stairs.

"I hope you are not too tired, Grandmama?" he asked.

"I have enjoyed every moment," the Dowager said. "To tell you the truth, dear boy, I am sick to death of being alone in bed."

The Marquis laughed and kissed her.

"I will give a dozen parties for you before you leave and there is certainly no hurry for you to do so."

"I have no intention of leaving until Flora says I am completely cured. That dear girl has worked miracles on me and I feel a different person since I came to the castle."

"You can stay as long as you like, Grandmama," the

Marquis replied. "I love having you here."

He kissed her again.

Then as he left her with her lady's maid, he noticed as he looked downstairs that Locadi was just crossing the hall.

That meant she was coming up to bed and he knew exactly what she was expecting.

The Marquis turned and hurried to his own room where his valet was waiting for him.

Only when he was undressed and wearing his long black robe did the man say,

"Is there anything else you require, my Lord?"

"No, thank you," the Marquis replied. "But please call me at six thirty. I wish to ride before breakfast, and you know there will be a great deal for me to do tomorrow."

"There will be indeed, my Lord," the valet agreed.

He left the room and the Marquis wondered desperately what he should do.

He knew that Locadi would be expecting him to visit her room, and if he did not she would undoubtedly come to his.

'I cannot do it,' he thought, 'I cannot face her and besides – '

He did not have to put it into words that he no longer desired her. In fact all he wanted was to avoid her.

He thought that if he slept in another room it would be impossible for her to find him, but then he was not so sure as she was using black magic.

He feared that, as she could direct her thoughts to him, she might in the same way be able to divine where he was sleeping.

In any event it would be degrading to be sleeping in a strange room while she roamed from room to room looking for him.

"What can I do? What the Devil can I do?"

The Marquis spoke the words aloud.

As he said them, he knew that Locadi was thinking of him and willing him towards her.

It was then that he was struck with a sudden idea.

If Locadi was using black magic which was evil, the only antidote would be something good.

For a moment he thought of riding over to see Flora and asking for her help, but then he told himself that was impossible. She must certainly not become involved in anything like his present situation.

She is pure, good and, he suspected, very innocent.

How could she understand women like Locadi who aroused passions in a man that were purely physical? And yet had nothing to do with the spiritual side of love.

'*Good and bad! Bad and good*!'

The words seemed to repeat themselves in his brain.

He conjectured that if he could not find white magic to fight the black, he must turn to something stronger than either of them.

Time was passing.

He was convinced that if he did not go to Locadi very shortly, she would come to him.

He felt sure she was just waiting like a wild animal crouching before it could strike.

She would realise very soon that his valet would have left him and the lights in that part of the house would be almost extinguished.

There would be no one to see her moving stealthily along the corridor towards the Master suite.

Swiftly the Marquis picked up a pillow and the eiderdown from his bed. Putting them over one arm and carrying a candle, he quietly left his room.

There was a secondary staircase which led to the ground floor and a night footman was on duty in the hall.

There was however no one to see him as he turned along a corridor which passed the drawing room and the study. As this corridor was not used at night, there were no lights except for the candle the Marquis was carrying.

Finally at the end of the passage he came to a door of Gothic design which led into the Chapel.

As he opened the door he was conscious of an atmosphere of sanctity and holiness which had been missing in the part of the castle he had just left.

The very beautiful Chapel was large enough to hold twenty people. It had been built in the age of Charles II and the carvings on the pews depicted angels and the coat of arms of the Wyns.

There was a gold cross studied with jewels on the altar and six tall candles in gold candlesticks.

Whether the Marquis was in residence or not, it had always been traditional that there should be flowers in the Chapel.

There were white flowers in pots on either side of the altar.

The family pew itself was long and wide and was built to seat four people comfortably, or more if they squeezed up.

It boasted comfortable well-padded cushions on the seats which were covered in red damask that matched the carpet which ran from the door to the altar.

The Marquis removed the key from outside the Chapel door and shutting the door behind him, he locked it.

Then he arranged his pillow on the pew and lay down spreading the eiderdown over him.

He had slept in far more uncomfortable places on his travels.

In fact he thought he was very comfortable.

When he closed his eyes he was quite certain that Locadi would not be able to penetrate his mind here in the Chapel, nor would she be able to intrude into his dreams.

As he lay there he was thinking of Flora and her herb garden.

The village people might think she practiced witchcraft, but they had no idea of what it meant in reality.

He had seen Locadi's eyes looking at him during dinner and afterwards when they were sitting in the drawing room. It was almost as if she was physically pulling him towards her.

However hard he tried not to recognise her, he felt as if her powers were engulfing him.

He blew out the candle and closing his eyes he prayed as he had not prayed for a long time.

It was quite a simple prayer.

He asked God to protect him from all that was evil, wrong and wicked. He also asked God to help him bring happiness and prosperity to his people and peace to himself.

He did not pretend that it was not his own fault that he had become so involved with Locadi.

He now believed that he needed a Power greater than himself to save him from what he accepted to be an evil and wicked snare.

'Please God help me,' he was praying over and over again until he fell asleep.

CHAPTER SIX

The Marquis was woken by the rising sun percolating through the stained glass windows of the Chapel.

He realised at once that he had slept peacefully and had not been disturbed by Locadi either in his dreams or in his thoughts.

He raised himself off the pew, stretched and picked up his pillow, eiderdown and candle.

Then as he looked at the altar he said a quiet prayer of gratitude that God had protected him during the night.

He climbed up the side staircase to his bedroom, where the clock showed that it would be another half-an-hour before he was due to be called and thought that he would lie on his bed for a while.

He turned to look at his bed and recognised that someone had slept in it.

He knew exactly what had happened. Locadi had, as he expected, come from her room to his and waited for him.

He supposed that she had only returned to her room at dawn to prevent his valet finding her.

'At least I won that round,' he thought to himself. Even so he was fearful of what the day might bring forth.

At six-thirty exactly his valet called him. When he was dressed he walked downstairs to visit to the stables, as he always preferred to go himself rather than order his horse brought round to him first thing in the morning.

Sometimes he would change his mind as to which horse he would ride and there were still some which he had not tried out since his return to the castle.

He was about to walk to the door nearest to the stables when a footman came hurrying towards him.

"Miss Romilly's waiting for your Lordship in the estate office, my Lord."

The Marquis raised his eyebrows.

He wondered what could have gone wrong and then thought that Flora must want to consult him about the plans for the party. But at *this* hour in the morning? He knew that today they would be very busy directing the workmen who would erect the tents. There would also be those who would set up the fireworks and yet another firm from whom he had ordered the tables and chairs.

He walked to the estate office which was actually on his way towards the stables.

As he entered Flora was standing at the writing-desk Mr. Potter had always used.

On the desk stood what looked like a large plant covered in wrapping.

"Good morning, Miss Flora," the Marquis greeted her, "you are very early."

"I wanted to catch you before you went riding," she said, "and to be able to speak to you alone."

The Marquis smiled.

"Is that usually so difficult?"

"Only sometimes," she answered, "but what I have brought you is rather special."

The Marquis looked at the parcel on the desk beside her.

"It is a mandrake plant. I thought we did not have one,

but then I remembered that some years ago Mama was given one."

"It sounds a strange present for your mother to be given," the Marquis remarked.

"Mama did not like it and she would not tolerate it in the herb garden. She planted it outside the walls and I have dug it up for you."

As she was speaking Flora started to undo the parcel.

When she had finished, the Marquis saw that it was a small mandrake which was not quite two feet high but was sprouting quite a number of leaves.

"It looks healthy enough," he said, "I thought you said it had to be planted under a gallows."

"That is what Papa has written in his book," Flora answered, "but this one has flourished in the field just beyond the herb garden."

She paused before she added a little shyly, "I did actually dig it – up in – the middle of the night."

"All I can say is that it is very kind of you, and I am extremely grateful. Now please tell me where I should put it."

"I think the best place, if you are not afraid of it, would be in your bedroom."

As the Marquis looked at her, she blushed and he guessed what she must be thinking.

"You are quite right," he said quietly, "that is where it should be."

"What I suggest is that by day you carry two leaves in your pockets. One on the right hand side and one on the left."

The Marquis thought that a month ago he would have laughed at such an idea, but now he took her seriously.

If the mandrake could really protect him from Locadi,

he was only too anxious to make full use of its powers.

He thought it was a strange looking plant. Then he remembered that he had seen illustrations of it in a book. He was not certain whether it was one of Mr. Romilly's or by some other author.

What he was absolutely sure about at the moment was that, if Flora believed in its powers, then he was prepared to do so too and he could only be grateful to her for having thought of him in his hour of need.

After a moment he said to Flora,

"I suppose you have come here on your horse."

"It was the easiest way to reach you so early."

"Then why do we not go for a ride together?" the Marquis enquired. "And if you would prefer to mount one of my horses for a change, you can come with me now to the stables."

Flora's eyes lit up.

"I would love to," she accepted gladly, "but we must not be long. The workmen are already arriving and if we are not here, they are certain to put the tents and everything else in the wrong place."

The Marquis laughed.

"Very well," he agreed, "let us hurry to the stables and enjoy our freedom until breakfast time."

Both the Marquis and Flora chose horses they had not ridden previously and because they found them hard to handle, they forgot all about the mandrake plant and Locadi.

After an exhilarating ride they returned to the castle just before eight o'clock.

The Marquis looking up at the windows as they crossed the bridge over the lake, spied someone watching them. Too late he remembered that Locadi's room overlooked the front of the house.

If he had possessed an ounce of sense, he thought, they would have ridden into the stables where they would not have been seen.

He instantly understood without being told that Locadi would be furious that he was riding out with Flora and it made it even worse that they had met so early in the morning.

However he did not say anything.

Once again he started wondering how he could persuade Locadi to depart for London.

He was uncomfortably aware that nothing would make her leave the castle unless accompanied by himself and this was definitely something he had no intention of doing.

The Marquis asked Flora to stay for breakfast, but she said she must go home and look after her father.

"I will come back as quickly as I can," she said. "Do watch what is happening beside the lake. You know how clumsy those people can be, and we want everything to be perfect for tomorrow."

"You have taken so much trouble over the party," the Marquis replied, "I shall be extremely annoyed if it is not all perfection."

Flora laughed.

"Hope for the best," she said, "and be prepared for the worst!"

As she finished speaking, she slipped down from the horse she had been riding and one of the grooms was waiting with her own horse for her ride home.

The Marquis lifted her again into the saddle.

This time she felt a quiver run through her which she had not felt earlier.

She was not certain what it was but it was strange.

She thought how strong he was.

116

The Marquis was thinking that she was so slim that it was like lifting a piece of thistledown onto the saddle.

She also looked, he noticed, exceedingly lovely.

As she rode away he knew that he had enjoyed his morning ride much more than if he had been alone.

Then with a sigh he walked into the castle.

He was thinking as he did so that Locadi was doubtless still watching him from behind the curtains at her window.

'I shall insist on her leaving on Monday,' he said to himself.

It was difficult however to think of an excuse as to why she should do so. He could hardly say there was not room for her when the castle was so big.

He was quite certain that she was determined to stay and she would therefore fight like a wild animal to prevent herself from being separated from him.

He ate his breakfast alone with these thoughts and they were not very happy ones.

Then he heard a noise outside as the first carriages came rumbling up the drive and he rushed out to supervise the workmen as Flora had asked him to do.

She joined him at ten o'clock and they were hard at work all morning.

The Marquis had engaged the local band to play and there had to be a stand for them. The men who were erecting the tents wanted to place them too near to each other.

The man who was delivering the chairs and tables wanted to leave before they were arranged in the tents, saying he had another job to do elsewhere.

It was at the last moment that the Marquis remembered he had not ordered any flowers for the tables.

When the gardener hurriedly brought them to the tents, there was no one to arrange them except Flora.

"If you had told me you were needing flowers," she said a little reproachfully, "there are two women in the village who can arrange them beautifully and who would have been delighted to help."

"Let me send for them," the Marquis suggested.

"Why not?" Flora replied, "I know there are a great many plants in the greenhouse which are just coming into bloom and which can be arranged around the bandstand."

"I had not thought of that," the Marquis said. "But let me first send for the women who will cope with the flowers."

He obtained their names from Flora and then walked to the stables to find Gower.

"I want you to send a groom to the village immediately," he ordered, "to ask Mrs. Smith and Mrs. Cosset to come up at once and help arrange the flowers on the tables where everyone will be eating tomorrow night."

"I can send young Ben," Gower said after a moment's pause. "But he ain't as good on a horse as I'd like him to be."

"What is wrong with Jimmy?" the Marquis enquired.

Jimmy had been a stable boy who had been employed at the castle before the Marquis had left to travel abroad. Potter had sacked him, but Gower had managed to attract him back.

"Now Jimmy's a different matter altogether," Gower said, "but he's gone to London."

"To London!" the Marquis exclaimed, "why has he gone there?"

"I thought it were on your orders, my Lord."

"I have not given any orders to one of our lads to go to London," the Marquis responded sharply.

"The lady came herself," Gower said. "Her told me it were very important that the letter her gives me should be in

London as quickly as possible."

There was no need for the Marquis to ask who the lady was.

There was only one lady in the castle, only one person, the Marquis surmised, who would have the cheek to send one of his staff to London without first seeking his permission.

*

There was no sign of Locadi until luncheon time.

The Marquis and Flora came in rather late to eat quickly in order to return to their work as soon as possible.

They found the Dowager had come downstairs and was talking to Locadi in the drawing room.

"How are you getting on, Ivor?" she asked. "I can see that you are both working very hard."

"There is so much to do." the Marquis replied, "and you have no idea how stupid these people can be unless they are properly supervised. Miss Flora and I have not dared to take our eyes off them for fear they should make a mess of things."

The Dowager laughed.

"It is always the same in the country. I can remember being exasperated in the old days when the band for my garden party was placed so that no one could hear them, and the tent where we were having tea nearly collapsed because the ropes were not fastened tightly enough."

Flora was amused.

"That is what I have been frightened of all morning, but I think that with the Marquis's help it will now be plain sailing."

While they were talking, the Marquis was aware that Locadi was gazing at him and there was an expression in her eyes which disturbed him.

He knew she was harbouring a hundred questions to ask him.

The first being why he had not come to her room last night.

As they finished luncheon he was wondering desperately how he could avoid being alone with her, as she was so obviously determined that he should be.

Finally when they left the dining room, he appealed to Flora,

"I suppose you could not have us to dinner with you tonight?

Flora looked at him in surprise.

"Are you really asking yourself to dine with Papa and me?"

"I am asking if I could bring my grandmother and Lady Marshall with me," he replied.

"Of course we will be delighted, but it is rather short notice so I must rush home and tell the cook to provide something very delicious for you."

"I would be content with bread and cheese," the Marquis said. "Anything rather than dine here."

As he spoke he considered that he was being somewhat indiscreet, but he was desperate.

"Do not worry," Flora said quickly. "I promise you it will be all right."

Later that evening he drove with his grandmother and Locadi to the *Four Gables*.

He could feel Locadi's anger and frustration flowing towards him like a tidal wave.

When he had told her at teatime that they were dining out, she said sharply,

"That is a ridiculous idea. What could be more pleasant than to dine here in this lovely castle?"

"I am afraid that I have already promised the Romillys that we would dine with them," he replied, "and I felt that both you and Grandmama would find it amusing."

"Amusing!" Locadi riposted scornfully. There was no need for her to say any more.

They enjoyed a pleasant and delicious dinner at which Mr. Romilly talked interestingly about his book and they drove back to the castle at about ten o'clock.

*

The Marquis was conscious of Locadi's determination to hold on to him tonight before he could disappear.

He managed to frustrate her first of all by escorting his grandmother upstairs to her bedroom.

Then he walked to his own room.

He undressed quickly and told his valet to go downstairs to where Locadi was waiting for him in the drawing room.

"Tell her I deeply regret it but I am suddenly feeling very unwell and cannot join her. It must be something I ate at dinner."

"I'll do that right away, my Lord," his valet said

"There is no need to come back. I also have a headache and want to get to sleep as quickly as possible."

"You must be well for the party tomorrow, my Lord."

"That is why it is so important that I should go to sleep now," the Marquis said firmly.

The valet hurried away to take the message to Locadi.

As soon as he had gone the Marquis walked to the Chapel as he had done the night before.

He had taken the mandrake from the estate office when he went upstairs before luncheon.

He had placed it in his bedroom.

As he left he felt that it would protect him against any evil spell that Locadi might wish to inflict on him.

When he reached the Chapel he lay down on the same pew he had slept on last night.

He felt the sanctity which seemed to come from the altar enveloping him.

In fact he fell asleep almost at once.

If he dreamed during the night, it was not of Locadi nor was he conscious of her the whole time he spent in the Chapel.

The next morning the Marquis knew there was so much to organise that it was really impossible for him to go for his usual ride.

He had told Flora that this was a pleasure that they would both have to forgo on Saturday morning and she had agreed with him.

"We are bound to find that there is something important we have forgotten," she said, "or that the tents have fallen down during the night! What I am really afraid of is that it might rain!"

"I think that is unlikely," the Marquis replied. "In fact I am rash enough to predict that we shall have a warm, pleasant day and a cloudless night with stars to add to the fireworks."

Flora laughed.

"The stars at least will cost you nothing."

"Stop worrying about the money. If this party is the success you have promised, it will make me a hero to my people, and that is what I want."

Flora laughed again and said,

"I am sure you will be successful, but I warn you that the small boys will be asking for fireworks every year after this, and you will find it very difficult to refuse them."

"Perhaps I shall enjoy them as much as they do," the Marquis replied.

"I know I shall," Flora said. "Like Lady Carson I have only seen fireworks once or twice in my life and these you have ordered are very, very special."

"I shall be very irritated if they are not," the Marquis asserted.

Because he sounded so serious, she smiled at him.

There was certainly a great deal still to do.

They ran out of flowers for one thing long before all the tables had been decorated. Flora had to send some of the helpers hurrying to *Four Gables* to ask the gardeners to pick everything they could find.

Fortunately the beds which her mother had planted were ablaze with flowers.

The boat which the Marquis was so keen to display had been lowered onto the lake.

It immediately nearly sank!

It was only saved by special attention from the estate carpenter – another man who had been brought back after being dismissed by Potter.

Neither Flora nor the Marquis could sit down for a moment. There was always someone asking for instructions or wanting some item which was invariably not obtainable.

*

At six-thirty the first guests began to arrive.

The Marquis felt as if he had been climbing the Himalayas and had crawled through the Pyramids as well.

Flora had returned home to change.

When she reappeared she was looking very pretty in a gown of blue muslin which matched her eyes. It had a full skirt which emphasized her tiny waist.

She was not wearing a hat but had entwined a wreath of blue flowers through her golden hair.

The Marquis thought that if she had appeared looking so exquisite at a ball in London, she would undoubtedly cause a sensation, especially amongst the young rakes who were extremely critical about their dancing partners.

He told himself that it would be a pity if she became spoilt by too much admiration and acclaim.

'That she is so unselfconscious and unaware of her own beauty,' he added, 'is her most attractive quality.'

"Papa is coming over later," Flora told him. "I think he really considers us all rather childish, because we are so excited about the fireworks and all the delicious things we expect to eat."

Mrs. Bowles had been cooking all day and Flora had been wise enough to find several women in the village who were good cooks. If they were given the necessary ingredients, they could prepare many of the cakes, sandwiches and other foods which were to be available for the hungry guests.

There were barrels of cider and beer and the Marquis commented dryly,

"If they wade through all this I shall expect them to sleep in the tents all night!"

"I would not be surprised at anything, but I know that it is going to be a wonderful party."

"I do hope you are right," the Marquis agreed. "If it is a failure after all the trouble we have taken, I shall be very angry."

"Do not worry," Flora declared. "It is going to be talked about and remembered for years, if not centuries. *The great party at Wyn Castle.* Can you not hear them chattering about it?"

"That is exactly what I want and I hope that by now we have thought of everything."

"Of course we have," Flora replied.

Johnny was among the first guests to arrive. He ran up to Flora calling excitedly,

"Miss Flora! Miss Flora! There's a boat on the lake with lights all over it. Can I go on it, please?" Flora crouched down so that she could put her arms around him.

"I am afraid you cannot," she said, "because if you do it might sink. But you must keep watching the boat because later in the evening fireworks will come out of it!"

"That'll be scrumptious," Johnny smiled.

"I tell you what we will do," said the Marquis who had been listening. "Tomorrow when we take the boat off the lake you shall see it on the ground and then you can climb into it if you want to."

"I'll really enjoy that," Johnny said, "It'll be very exciting."

He ran off to tell the other children what he was going to do and the Marquis said,

"That too was what I wanted to do, although I was much older than Johnny when the boat first appeared."

"And did you get into it?" Flora asked.

"I was too big," the Marquis replied. "But I always felt I had missed out by not going in the Fairy boat which could sail without anyone propelling it, a blaze of lights on the lake."

"It is certainly very effective, but I am quite certain I would not have thought of it as an attraction if you had not remembered it."

"You have thought of a great many other ideas and I know the children will love them all."

There were swings and slides and even a coconut shy

in another part of the garden. Flora could hear the shrieks of excitement from the children as they played around them.

More and more people appeared.

A little later the Chief Constable and Lady Carson arrived with their son.

"I was beginning to think," the Marquis said as he shook Lady Carson's hand, "that you had forgotten about us."

"It is my husband's fault," she responded. "Some people came to see him just as we were leaving. I can assure you it is very difficult being married to a policeman."

The Marquis laughed.

As Lady Carson moved away to talk to Flora, the Chief Constable whispered into the Marquis's ear,

"I have brought several of my men with me. I have heard that there are some strange people from London in the village and if there is to be any trouble, we will deal with it."

"Trouble?" the Marquis queried. "I was not anticipating anything like that."

"You never know on occasions like this," the Chief Constable replied. "As everyone has been talking about your party, there are sure to be a number of crooks who will try to get in on the act, so to speak."

"I know what you mean, but I am hoping that nothing will happen."

"Just tell your staff in the house to see that the windows are all locked and also the doors to the main rooms. I do not want you to lose any of your famous pictures."

"Certainly not," the Marquis agreed, "and of course you are quite right that it is better to be prepared for anything on these sort of occasions."

"That is what I have always thought," the Chief Constable answered. "Do not worry, my men will deal with any problems."

The Marquis thanked him and took him into the tent where there was a special table reserved for his guests.

His grandmother was already present and a little later the Carsons sat down to talk to her.

The band outside was playing the tunes that everyone enjoyed.

The food was excellent and Flora joined them for a short while before slipping away to see if the children, who were still playing on the slides and the swings, wanted something to eat.

"She thinks of everyone," the Dowager told the Carsons. "In fact she is the sweetest girl I have ever met, and I am eternally grateful to her for the way she has treated me with her magic herbs."

"She is certainly a great asset to the County," Lady Carson commented.

They had finished eating and it was almost time for the fireworks to begin.

The Marquis excused himself to see if he could find Flora.

By now there was an enormous crowd of people milling around the lake watching the boat and waiting for the fireworks to start.

Everyone was in very good spirits, laughing and talking.

The Marquis thought that the beer and the cider had certainly contributed to the gaiety of the evening.

There was no sign of Flora.

He walked down as far as the swings but the smaller children were not there. He thought that she must have taken them into one of the tents.

Slowly he began to retrace his steps.

Then there was a whizz and a bang and the first firework shed a hundred shining stars over the lake.

It was followed by another and yet another.

Now the children were shouting with delight and even some of the older people were joining in. This was what they had been waiting for.

The Marquis thought that with the moon shining above and the sky full of stars nothing could look more glamorous.

However he still could not find Flora. He looked into both the tents which were now emptying rapidly. The band was playing softly as a background to the noise of the fireworks.

There was also, the Marquis was suddenly aware, no sign of Locadi.

He had not missed her while they were eating in the tent. He felt that she had been bored with the party from the very beginning, but would doubtless come and watch the fireworks if nothing else.

He would not have been at all surprised if she was sulking in the castle as she had not been able to be in touch with him all day.

He was convinced that the mandrake leaves in both his pockets were protecting him. He had not been so uncomfortably conscious of her today as he had been yesterday.

He was still however thinking of Flora.

Now as he walked amongst the crowd with everyone's heads turned towards the sky, he was overcome by a strange feeling that she needed him.

It was almost as if she was calling to him.

This struck him as being very odd.

Where before he had been aware of Locadi, now it was Flora who was in his mind.

It was almost as if he could hear her calling to him,

"*Save me – save me!*"

'I must be demented,' he told himself. 'First I imagine that Locadi is beside me and now I can almost hear Flora's voice pleading with me.'

He wondered if he was going mad.

He walked towards the castle, for a moment turning his back on the fireworks.

It was then that he saw running round the side of the Norman Tower a small boy whom he recognized as Johnny.

He was crying loudly and holding his hands up to his eyes.

The Marquis hurried towards him.

"What is the matter, Johnny?" he asked.

"He – hit me. The – bad man – hit me," Johnny cried pitifully.

The Marquis picked him up into his arms.

"Now tell me what has happened and stop crying because I want you to watch the fireworks."

"The – bad men took – away Miss – Flora," Johnny sobbed. "They put a – big black bag over – her head and – when I tried to go with her they – hit me – they hit me – very, very hard and it – hurts."

The words came out almost incoherently.

The Marquis was listening in astonishment and then he asked,

"Where have the bad men taken Miss Flora?"

Johnny threw out his arm to indicate the way he had come.

"To – the woods," he said.

"Miss Flora was showing me – the fountain and they – carried her – away."

The Marquis could hardly believe it.

Then as if he could hear Flora telling him that it was true, he looked round.

He saw a village woman whom he knew standing watching the fireworks.

He carried Johnny up to her and said, "Johnny has been hurt. Please look after him."

"Hurt, my Lord? I'll see to him at once," the woman answered.

She put her arms round Johnny and the Marquis started to run in the direction of the first tent.

He remembered that when they came out from dinner there had been a seat outside it.

The Chief Constable had sat to watch the fireworks in comfort and when the Marquis reached the tent he saw to his relief that he was still there.

The noise of the fireworks was now almost deafening and he bent over the back of the seat shouting,

"Please come at once, I think Miss Flora has been kidnapped."

The Chief Constable looked up to see if he was joking and then he repeated.

"*Kidnapped*?"

"Some men have taken her away and I think I know where they have gone."

The Chief Constable jumped up and without speaking to his wife who had not been listening to what they had been saying, joined the Marquis.

They moved swiftly across the grass and on to the gravel courtyard.

"You believe," the Chief Constable asked, "that she has been taken away from here?"

"Yes, I am almost certain," the Marquis replied, "that they have taken her to the Chapel in the woods.

The Chief Constable put his hand into his pocket and drew out a police whistle. He placed it to his lips and it made a shrill sound.

The Marquis thought that no one would notice it above the noise of the fireworks, the music of the band and the cries of the crowd.

But almost instantly three policemen followed by a fourth came running up to the Chief Constable.

As they reached him the Marquis turned and started to walk very quickly towards the Tower. They skirted round it and on to the green lawn where the fountain was playing.

As they did so he was certain he could hear Flora calling him again, this time more frantically. He did not stop to wonder why or how this was possible.

He just knew that she needed him urgently and it was imperative that he should reach her as quickly as possible.

The Chief Constable was following him and the four policemen were close behind.

The green lawn came to an end and there were the first rhododendron bushes. Beyond them were the silver birch trees of which the shrubbery mostly consisted.

There were twisting paths winding between the trees.

Then as the Marquis ran through the trees he became aware he could hear faintly but distinctly, the sound of voices.

They came, he guessed, from the Chapel which had been built by his ancestor.

He had no idea why Flora should be there. But his instinct told him that she *was* there and at this moment she wanted him desperately.

CHAPTER SEVEN

Flora could not believe what was happening to her.

She knew that she was being carried by a man across the lawn.

Something thick and dark had been pulled over her head so that it was impossible for her to scream.

She was hardly able to breathe.

She had gone to find the children to find out if they had enjoyed playing and had enough to eat before the fireworks started.

She found that most of them had left the swings with the exception of Johnny.

"Come along, Johnny," she had urged, "I want you to have some food."

"Not hungry," Johnny had said firmly.

"I think you will be when you see the delicious dishes which are on the table," Flora replied.

Then as they were walking away from the swings she said, "I know what I will show you. We were talking about it the other day – the big fountain here at the castle."

"I like fountains," Johnny agreed excitedly.

"I know you do," Flora answered. "And this is a very big one, much bigger than the one in my herb garden."

She took him around the side of the Norman Tower to

the lawn in the centre of which stood the fountain.

It looked particularly beautiful as Flora had already seen for herself. The moonlight and the stars were reflected in the rise and fall of the water.

Johnny clapped his hands with delight.

Flora explained to him how the water came out of the centre of the fountain.

Then he was looking for the goldfish swimming amongst the water lilies in the bowl.

Quite suddenly something heavy was thrown over Flora's head and someone picked her up in his arms.

She tried to cry out but for the moment she was too stunned to make a sound.

She heard Johnny scream and was afraid of what had happened to him.

By then the man who was carrying her was hurrying over the grass. She could feel when he left it and started to climb the twisting path which led through the shrubbery.

It was at this moment that she wondered if he was taking her to the Chapel, and if so why?

This was all so bewildering because it was so unexpected and so violent and Flora was becoming very frightened.

Next the man who was carrying her stopped suddenly and she became aware for the first time that there was another man behind him.

She heard his footsteps also come to a standstill and he must have opened the door of the little hut which adjoined the Chapel.

Flora guessed that she was being carried into the room which the sixth Earl had built for his own use beside the Chapel.

She had visited the room so often that she knew

exactly what it contained. The narrow hard bed where he slept was in one corner, there were two large chests and at the end of the room a round table on which the Earl ate his meals.

Now at last the man who was carrying Flora hauled her down from his shoulder.

As her feet touched the floor she felt somehow relieved.

Was this just a joke she wondered?

Then she felt his hands pulling at the dark hood over her head.

He drew it away and as Flora opened her eyes to her astonishment she found that she was facing Locadi.

"What is – happening?" Flora managed to stammer. "Why have – I been brought – here?"

"You will learn the answer soon enough," Locadi answered in a sinister voice.

She looked over Flora's shoulder at the man behind her.

"I will see to her now," she ordered. "Get everyone ready."

"We will not be long," he replied, "the others were preparing everything when I left."

"Yes, I know that," Locadi snapped.

Flora looked from one to the other. She thought the man, who was tall and dark, had a very unpleasant face. He was not young and there was something cruel in his expression.

Also something else to which she could not put a name.

As if to obey Locadi, he walked across the room and pulled open the door which Flora knew led into the Chapel.

As he did so a strong and sickly scent of incense wafted towards her and it was quite different, Flora thought, from any incense she had ever smelt before.

As he closed the door behind him, Locadi ordered in a sharp tone,

"*Undress!*"

"What do you mean – ? Why have you had me – brought here? I do not – understand."

"You will learn everything in due course," Locadi snarled. "Just do as I tell you at once."

"I do not know what you are talking about and I refuse to take off my clothes."

To her absolute amazement, Locadi brought forward a revolver she had been hiding behind her back.

Flora looked at it in sheer disbelief.

"Now you listen to what I have to say," Locadi screamed. "If you do not do what I tell you, I shall shoot, not to kill you but at your feet. I will damage them so that you will never walk again."

"You must be – mad to be saying this – to me," Flora cried.

As she looked at Locadi, she saw the pupils of her eyes were dark and dilated and she thought that she must be drunk.

Then she realised that the round table at the other end of the room was piled with the remains of food and a large number of empty wine bottles.

However as Flora looked again at Locadi, her appearance was so strange that she was now sure she was drugged.

"Why do – you want – me to take – off my – clothes?" she managed to blurt out.

"Do as I tell you," Locadi snapped, "or I will cripple you and you will find it very painful."

'She is mad, completely mad,' Flora told herself.

She was so extremely frightened, but felt that it would be best to obey what Locadi was ordering her to do.

She took off the pretty blue gown she was wearing and placed it on the bed.

Then slowly, hoping that Locadi would allow her to stop, she took off her petticoat.

As she knew the older woman was watching her every movement, she removed her other clothes.

"I – must have – something to cover – myself with," she stuttered.

With a disdainful gesture Locadi picked up a large piece of thin muslin which was lying on one of the chairs.

It might have been a table cloth.

She handed it to Flora who quickly wrapped it around her naked body.

Then Locadi said in the same aggressively ominous tone,

"If you scream, or try to run away, or do anything except what you are told to do, I will shoot at your feet."

"*But why?* Why are – you doing – this to me?"

"You will find out soon enough that you do not cross Locadi. Ivor is mine and always will be and you are going to discover that *my* magic is stronger than *yours*. You are the key I need to capture Ivor's heart forever".

She walked across the room to the door of the Chapel and pulled it open. As she did so Flora noticed for the first time the garment she was wearing.

It was a strange robe of many colours which was marked with unusual signs.

Flora felt that she ought to be able to recognise them.

Locadi's feet were bare and it suddenly struck Flora that beneath her robe she too was naked.

"What is – happening?" she asked frantically. "What – can all – this mean?"

As the strong smell of the incense coming from the Chapel filled the room, Flora had a terrifying thought.

Before she could say anything, the man who had carried her from the garden came in through the door. He was looking even larger and more menacing than earlier and now he too was wearing a robe not unlike the one worn by Locadi.

He walked towards Flora and instinctively she tried to shrink away from him.

He merely picked her up in his arms again and carried her into the Chapel.

It was so frightening that Flora wanted to scream.

However she forced herself to be silent because Locadi still held the revolver in her hand.

Now as they entered the Chapel, she became aware that six other people were present and they were all men.

They began to intone a chant which Flora thought sounded like prayers, but if they were, they were unlike any prayers that she had ever heard except that they were in Latin.

Then to her horror she recognised several of the names they were saying. She had read of them in her father's books.

Adramelech, the God of murder, *Moloch* the fatalist who devoured children and *Nisroch* the God of hatred.

Flora closed her eyes but she could feel that the man carrying her had reached the altar – the beautiful marble altar which had come from Italy.

Now he was laying her down on the altar.

When he had done so, he pulled away the piece of cloth Locadi had given her.

She was lying naked on the altar.

As the horror of her plight swept through her, she knew if she looked round what she would see.

The men in the Chapel were now speaking in English and she heard them chanting,

"*Beelzebub, Adramelech, Lucifer*, come to us! Masters of Darkness – we implore thee! Satan, *we are thy slaves*! Come! Come! Illuminate us with thy presence!"

Before they uttered the last words, because she needed to know the worst, Flora opened her eyes and now she could see all too clearly what she had suspected.

Above her was the beautiful gold cross which had always stood on the altar, but it was upside down.

There were six black candles immediately over her and almost touching the ceiling was the image of a huge bat with its wings outstretched.

She could see its beady eyes, its pointed nose and the hooks at the end of its great wings.

Flora knew at once that it was the emblem of Satan and that she was taking part in the Black Mass.

She felt it could not possibly be true.

She had read about the Black Mass in the history books and in her father's writings.

Catherine de Medici had used black magic in an attempt to capture the love of her husband, the King of France, who she believed was under a spell put on him by Diane de Poitiers.

Quite recently in France, Flora remembered her father telling her that there had been Papal denunciations against those who dabbled in the occult and especially in black magic.

How was it possible and how could it be true that a black magic service was taking place at the castle?

She was to be the sacrifice to Satan.

She had read all about it in her father's book that human sacrifices were made by those who worshipped the Devil.

Flora had thought vaguely that the victim was usually a child or an animal. Her father had hinted that there were other rituals that were perpetrated on a woman, but she was not certain what they were.

Now the prayers, if that was what they were, had started again.

Moving only her eyes but not her head, Flora could see arms covered in robes embroidered with strange Satanic symbols and those arms were beseeching the bat hanging above her.

There came to her mind something that her father had written,

'*Before a Black Mass starts, contrary to the custom of Christians who fast, those taking part eat and drink excessively.*'

Flora wondered if the men were all drugged as was Locadi.

Because she was desperately afraid of what the wicked woman would do to her, she opened her eyes once again.

Locadi was standing at the side of the altar, and she too was praying in the same manner as the men.

Flora understood that they were calling down Satan into their midst and imploring a host of devils. She recognised some of the names they were chanting and that they were all the embodiment of evil.

"*Beliah* in eternal revolt and anarchy! *Ashtaroth, Nehamah, Astarte* in debauchery!"

Now she was really terrified.

Once again the men and Locadi were calling to Satan to join them.

In her terror Flora wondered if Satan really appeared to those who called on him.

Then she remembered she was in a Chapel dedicated to God and it was only God who could help her.

'*Help me* – please help me God,' she cried out in her heart.

Then she called out to the Marquis.

She thought, just as she could read his thoughts, if she cried out to him he might just be able to hear her.

She was desperately afraid of what would happen to her when she was to be sacrificed to Satan.

She felt that at any moment the man standing over her might touch her, as he was very obviously the High Priest.

Very soon now she would feel his hands on her naked body.

Every time she opened her eyes even a fraction, she could see his hands projecting from his Satanic robe.

'Help me – come to me – save me. Oh, Ivor – Ivor, *save me*!'

She almost felt as if she was saying the words aloud because they flowed so intensely from her heart and her soul.

She was praying to God.

"Please God – let him hear me. Please – God send him – to me."

She became even more frightened because she could hear that the chanting was growing louder and louder.

It was as if the men had lost control and in their intensity were almost shouting.

"Come to us O, Master of Darkness – come to us. We are waiting."

It was at this moment that Flora was sure that they intended to kill her.

She saw, because she could not help looking, that the High Priest was holding his hands over her once again, but now they were turned downwards.

She knew they were exercising mesmeric and hypnotic power over her body and this was the signal for them to offer her as a sacrifice.

"*Ivor – Ivor!*"

Despite her fear of Locadi, the words came audibly from between her lips.

Then suddenly there was the crash of a door bursting open and she heard the Marquis's voice demanding furiously,

"What the hell is going on here?"

His voice rang out to the rafters and at that moment one of the policemen strode into the Chapel just in front of the Marquis.

Locadi raised her revolver and shot at him.

There was a loud explosion.

The bullet missed the policeman by an inch and buried itself in the lintel of the door.

There was another shot as one of the other policemen who was behind him shot directly at Locadi.

He aimed for her arm but she had moved forward as if to gain advantage over her opponent.

The bullet entered her breast.

She fell over with a scream and pandemonium broke out.

The men who had been chanting were all screaming as the police rushed towards them.

The Marquis ran with them.

The High Priest standing over Flora seemed bemused by what was occurring all around him.

The Marquis swiftly caught him a hard blow on the point of his chin which knocked him over backwards and he fell to the floor with a groan.

The Marquis did not wait to see if he was conscious or unconscious.

He picked Flora up off the altar and carried her through the door into the room from which she had just come.

All the policemen and the Chief Constable were by this time grappling with the Satanists in the centre of the Chapel.

As the Marquis carried Flora into the room, he pressed his back against the door and closed it.

Then he asked her,

"Are you all right?"

"I – prayed to – you to come – and save – me,"

Flora murmured incoherently.

"*I heard you*," the Marquis replied. Thank God you have not been harmed by those monsters!"

He could feel her naked body trembling against him.

There were tears in her eyes but she was not crying.

He looked at her for a long moment as if to make sure that she was not injured in any way.

Then very gently his lips touched hers.

It was a very soft and gentle kiss.

He saw Flora's eyes open and a light in them which had not been there before.

"You have been so brave in resisting their evil, but now we must get out of here as quickly as possible," the Marquis urged. "No one must know what has happened here."

"No – of course – not."

He saw her clothes lying on the bed.

"Can you dress yourself,?" he asked. "Or shall I help you?"

"I – can – manage," Flora replied.

She was thinking of his kiss and the strange feeling it had given her. It had somehow swept away the nightmare of everything she had just been through.

"Hurry," the Marquis said as he put her down very carefully on the floor.

She moved towards the bed.

As she did so, the Marquis pulled one of the chests in front of the door so that no one could come in unexpectedly. It was a heavy chest, carved locally at the time the Chapel was built and inset with stones.

When he had finished the Marquis asked without turning round,

"Are you nearly ready?"

"Perhaps you could – do up my gown please."

He walked towards her realising that she had dressed as quickly as he had hoped, but her gown did up only at the back.

He attended to the buttons and arranged the wreath tidily on her head.

"We must go back now," he said, "and no one will know all this has happened. The Chief Constable will see to that."

"Was he – with you?" Flora asked.

"He was indeed and he entered the Chapel at the same time as I did and might easily have been shot."

Flora said nothing and the Marquis walked towards the door and pulled it open.

"Can you walk?" he asked.

"I will try."

The Marquis did not ask any more questions but merely picked her up in his arms.

As he did so she thought how very different it felt being carried away by him from the way she had been bundled by the repulsive High Priest.

Now in the Marquis's arms she felt secure and safe.

The horror and fear of what had just occurred was slipping away as if it had been a bad dream.

He walked down the narrow path which led to the lawn and then across the grass.

Flora thought perhaps he would take her back to the fireworks, as she could still hear explosions and the cheers of the crowd as each new display glittered over the lake.

The Marquis however took her in by one of the doors at the back of the castle.

He opened it without putting her down. Still carrying her he took her down a dark passage with the only light coming from the broader corridor at the end.

Flora wondered where they were going, but somehow it did not seem to matter.

Then they were in a very dark passage where she felt that only the Marquis would know his way.

He pushed open another door and they entered a room which was dark although there was a faint light coming through an uncurtained window.

The Marquis put her down gently on what she felt was a bench.

"There is something I want to show you," he said quietly.

She wondered what it was, but for the moment she felt too limp to ask questions.

He had found her and he had saved her. That was all that mattered.

The miracle had been that he had heard her calling him when she was encompassed by evil.

'He might have been an Archangel from Heaven,' Flora thought to herself.

Then she remembered that he had kissed her.

She thought it was the most wonderful thing that had ever happened to her and she knew now that she loved him.

She had loved him for a long time, ever since she had discovered that he was so kind, sympathetic and understanding.

But she had not realised it was love.

She loved him and, because she was now in the darkness, she was suddenly afraid that he had left her.

Then she became aware that he was lighting a candle at the end of the room.

He lit another and Flora realised that she was in the Chapel in the castle which she had not visited for some time.

The Marquis lit six candles.

Now she could see how beautiful the castle Chapel looked with its gold cross the right way up.

There was no hideous bat hovering above it, only the stained glass windows through which just a little light was shining from the moon and the stars.

There was the scent not of incense but of flowers, which decorated the altar and there were large vases standing on either side.

The Marquis came back to her and when he reached her he pulled her gently out of the chair until she was standing.

"You have been through a most unpleasant and wicked experience," he said, "and I thought you would like to come here as it would help you to forget it. We can also say a prayer of thankfulness to God that I reached you in time."

"I am – so very – grateful," Flora stammered. At the same time it was difficult to speak because what the Marquis had said had touched her heart.

Tears had come into her eyes.

'Could any man,' she asked herself, 'be so wonderful and so understanding? Could any other man have remembered that the only antidote to evil is good?'

The Marquis took her up the short aisle.

Then they knelt down on the steps which led up to the altar.

He did not relinquish her hand and Flora held tightly on to his as she shut her eyes.

'Thank you God – thank you,' she prayed silently. 'You sent Ivor to – save me and I – thank you from the depths of my soul.'

She sensed that the Marquis was saying the same prayer.

Then as he rose and pulled her up beside him he put his arms round her.

He felt her quiver and she looked up at him questioningly.

His mouth came down on hers and he kissed her.

At first gently and then as he felt the softness and innocence of her lips, his kisses became more demanding, more possessive.

To Flora it was as if the Heavens had opened and the angels themselves were singing with joy and happiness.

She knew now that the ecstasy she was feeling was unlike anything she had ever known before.

This was the love which she had wanted all her life but had feared that it would be impossible to find.

'I love you, I love you,' she wanted to say.

The Marquis was saying it with his kisses.

The tightness of his arms which held her close against him made it real and not a dream.

She thought that nothing could be more glorious, as if God Himself was smiling on them and giving them His special blessing.

After what seemed a long time, the Marquis raised his head.

"I love you, my darling," he declared.

"As I love you," Flora whispered. "I did not know – it was love, I just knew that you were – wonderful.

"The Marquis smiled.

"That is just what I want you to go on thinking. How soon will you marry me, my precious? Because I cannot live without you."

Flora stared at him.

"Are – you," she paused for a moment, "asking – me to be – your – wife?"

"I want you to marry me at once, as quickly as possible," the Marquis stated. "We have so much to do and we must do it together as I no longer wish to be alone."

He felt as he spoke that just as he had saved Flora from an unspeakable and ghastly experience, she had equally saved him from Locadi.

She was his destiny as a pure catalyst for the triumph of good over evil and Flora's magic could only come from God, Mother Nature and the spirituality of her own soul.

She deserved the title of the *White Witch* by the locals, but her goodness shone like the stars and would always overcome the wicked scheming of Locadi and her black magic.

There might be other evils threatening him, but if she was with him he knew he would be safe.

The two leaves from the mandrake plant were still in his pockets and he wanted them to remain there forever – they had protected him against Locadi and guided him to save Flora from a terrible fate.

"And when will you marry me?" he asked.

"At once – tonight – this very moment," Flora cried.

The Marquis laughed.

"That is what I want to hear, my lovely one. We will not wait and our wedding will be the Vicar's first service when he returns to the Vicarage next week."

"Can we be – married here in this – beautiful Chapel?" Flora enquired.

"It is what I would love, but perhaps you want a grand wedding."

"I would love a very quiet wedding with just you and Papa there."

"And I want just my grandmother to be present," the Marquis said, "so that is all settled!"

He kissed her again before asking her,

"Are you brave enough to come back to the party? I think it is essential that we should be seen in case there are any rumours or speculation about what has happened."

"Yes, of course we must go back," Flora agreed.

They walked down the little aisle hand in hand and out through the door which led to the side of the courtyard. As they did so they heard a wild cry of excitement.

The fireworks on the other side of the lake spelt out *'Goodnight and Good luck'*.

It was the end of the party.

The Marquis noted to his satisfaction that no one would have noticed that he and Flora had been away for any length of time.

As the fireworks died out, the band played '*God Save the Queen*', and everyone stood to attention.

By this time the Marquis and Flora had almost reached the bandstand.

As the last note died away from the singing of the National Anthem, someone at the back of the crowd shouted,

"Three cheers for his Lordship!"

Everyone cheered and the Marquis stepped up onto the bandstand.

"I want to thank you all," he said, "for coming here tonight. I want you to understand that this is the beginning of a new era on the estate. It is to be one of hard work, progress and, I hope, happiness for everyone."

He paused before continuing,

"We can only be successful if you all help me to develop new ideas and new interests in order to bring prosperity us all of us."

There were more cheers and the Marquis resumed,

"As the future is such a demanding proposition, I felt I could not manage it alone. Therefore I want to tell you that I am the luckiest man in the world because Flora Romilly, whom you all know and love, has promised to be my wife."

There were audible gasps.

Then everyone burst into even louder cheers, which were very different to the ones they had given before.

The men waved their hats and the women their handkerchiefs.

The children rushed down to the front of the bandstand so that they could be close to Flora.

She joined the Marquis and they both waved and smiled at the ovation they were receiving, and then they stepped down to walk amongst the crowd, shaking hands with practically everyone.

There were the older members of the staff, who told the Marquis they had known him since he was a boy and were so glad that he had returned home.

The women who had been cured and looked after by Flora had a great deal to say to her.

It took a long time but it was quite obvious that no one intended to leave until they had shaken hands with both the Marquis and his future wife.

Finally some of the older women started to walk slowly down the drive and the children, who were still too excited to be sleepy, were dragged away by their mothers who wanted to take them home to bed.

At last the band packed up and the Marquis and Flora started to walk back to the castle.

As they did so they saw the Chief Constable waiting for them. A little apprehensively the Marquis walked up to him.

"What has happened?" he asked.

The Chief Constable smiled.

"Seven men," he said, "have been charged with trespassing, breaking and entering with the intention of stealing. They have been taken to the local Police Station and that is all that will be said when they appear in front of the magistrates."

The Marquis gave a sigh of relief.

"However," the Chief Constable continued, "we have discovered that they belong to a particular Church in London and I am quite sure that it will not function any longer."

"And Lady Marshall?" the Marquis asked in a low voice.

"Her Ladyship," the Chief Constable responded, "suffered an unfortunate accident with a faulty revolver. It is with deep regret that we have to report that she died on the way to the hospital."

For a moment the Marquis was speechless before saying,

"How can I thank you for your kindness?"

"You can thank me," the Chief Constable replied, "by fulfilling everything you have just described so eloquently to your people. I want this County to be known as one of the quietest and most prosperous in the whole country."

"We will certainly help you achieve that aim," Flora said.

"I am sure you will," the Chief Constable replied. "Now I must congratulate you both, and will you allow me to say that I have never known two people whom I thought were better suited to each other."

"That is exactly what we think," the Marquis said smiling.

He shook the Chief Constable by the hand and then as he wanted to be quite sure there could be no mistake he said,

"I suppose you can trust your men not to talk."

"I would trust them with my life. No one will ever hear of what actually occurred tonight in the Earl's Chapel."

"That is just what I was hoping," the Marquis said, "and thank you so much again."

The Chief Constable drove off and by this time there was practically no one left.

The Marquis drew Flora into the house. "I am never going to let you out of my sight in case you vanish again. I will send a servant to tell your father where you are and to bring back your clothes."

The lights had been partially extinguished and there was only the night footman on duty in the hall.

The Marquis gave his orders and they walked up the stairs side by side.

When they reached a bedroom next to the Master Suite, the Marquis opened the door, followed her inside and lit the candles.

"I want you to go to sleep, my darling one, and forget everything that happened tonight except that you promised to marry me and we are going to be very happy together."

"I am still afraid it is just a dream," Flora said. "You are so wonderful that I am still half afraid that you will vanish into the sky."

She gave a little laugh and added,

"I thought when you rescued me you were like the Archangel Michael, and now I am frightened of losing you."

"You will never lose me, my *White Witch*," the Marquis sighed. "I fought against loving you because I have suffered from women in a way I do not want to explain and thought that I would never marry until I grew old. Your magic has cast a spell over my heart that can never be broken."

He put out his hand to touch her cheek very gently as he said,

"But you are so beautiful and so perfect that it is impossible not to want you at once for myself and myself alone."

"That is exactly what you will have," Flora replied, "because there is no other man in the world who is as marvellous as you are."

The Marquis drew her closer to him.

"I love you. I love you!" he said. "I know there is so much for us to do together but I too want you all to myself. That is what we will be when we go abroad."

"You know that I would love to travel with you. You remember I told you that I thought I should only be able to travel in my mind."

"I remember everything you have ever said to me. You are going to travel with me and we will explore strange lands and strange people as well as ourselves."

"Are you quite certain that I will not bore you?"

"That would be utterly impossible. There is so much about you that I want to learn and I hope too there is a lot about me that will keep you interested."

"I cannot imagine anything more exciting. Oh, darling, darling Ivor, let us get married quickly. I cannot bear to be parted from you for a second."

"We will be married on Tuesday or Wednesday at the latest," he said, "and I shall be thinking in the mean time where we will go for our honeymoon."

"We cannot go too far," Flora said quickly, "because there is so much to be accomplished here."

"Wherever we go," the Marquis replied, "we shall be alone and together and that is what I want, because I have so much to teach you, my precious one, about love."

"That will – be very – exciting!" Flora whispered.

"I intend it to be," he sighed. "But you also have a great deal more to teach me about people, how to deal with them and how to make them happy."

Flora gave a little laugh.

"That is certainly going to take a long time."

"Just is what I thought," the Marquis said, "so, my beloved, there will be no chance of our ever being bored with each other because we have so much to achieve together."

He kissed her again.

Now his kisses were not only demanding and possessive but also passionate.

He kissed her until they both felt as if the ecstasy within them was carrying them up into the sky.

They were touching the stars that Flora had always

loved.

The light of the moon enveloped them and joined the ecstasy in their hearts.

"I – love you – love – you," Flora murmured and the Marquis was saying the same.

There had been many difficulties in his life but now he had found what he was seeking.

It was not in the Himalayas or in the desert or in any strange country but right here at home.

It was more valuable than any precious stone that he might have found in the East.

It was the gem of life combined with love. Something which had inspired mankind since the dawn of civilization.

It was searched for arduously in this world but was actually to be found in the world beyond.

It was the love that was the very Spirit of God. A love which when given to a man and a woman made them part of the Divine.